Titles by Jayne Anne Krentz

LOST & FOUND

AMARYLLIS

ZINNIA

ORCHID

CHARMED

SOFT FOCUS

DAWN IN ECLIPSE BAY

BRIDAL
JITTERS

BRIDAL JITTERS

Jayne Castle

BERKLEY BOOKS, NEW YORK

THE BERKLEY PUBLISHING GROUP
Published by the Penguin Group
Penguin Group (USA) Inc.
375 Hudson Street, New York, New York 10014, USA
Penguin Group (Canada), 90 Eglinton Avenue East, Suite 700, Toronto, Ontario M4P 2Y3, Canada
(a division of Pearson Penguin Canada Inc.)
Penguin Books Ltd., 80 Strand, London WC2R 0RL, England
Penguin Group Ireland, 25 St. Stephen's Green, Dublin 2, Ireland (a division of Penguin Books Ltd.)
Penguin Group (Australia), 250 Camberwell Road, Camberwell, Victoria 3124, Australia
(a division of Pearson Australia Group Pty. Ltd.)
Penguin Books India Pvt. Ltd., 11 Community Centre, Panchsheel Park, New Delhi—110 017, India
Penguin Group (NZ), Cnr. Airborne and Rosedale Roads, Albany, Auckland 1310, New Zealand
(a division of Pearson New Zealand Ltd.)
Penguin Books (South Africa) (Pty.) Ltd., 24 Sturdee Avenue, Rosebank, Johannesburg 2196,
South Africa

Penguin Books Ltd., Registered Offices: 80 Strand, London WC2R 0RL, England

Previously published in the anthology *Charmed*, published by The Berkley Publishing Group.

This is a work of fiction. Names, characters, places, and incidents either are the product of the author's imagination or are used fictitiously, and any resemblance to actual persons, living or dead, business establishments, events, or locales is entirely coincidental.

BRIDAL JITTERS

A Berkley Book / published by arrangement with the author

PRINTING HISTORY
Berkley edition / October 2005

ISBN: 0-425-20864-8

BERKLEY®
Berkley Books are published by The Berkley Publishing Group,
a division of Penguin Group (USA) Inc.,
375 Hudson Street, New York, New York 10014.
BERKLEY is a registered trademark of Penguin Group (USA) Inc.
The "B" design is a trademark belonging to Penguin Group (USA) Inc.

PRINTED IN THE UNITED STATES OF AMERICA

10 9 8 7 6 5 4 3 2 1

BRIDAL JITTERS

One

"So, is it true what they say about ghost-hunters?" Adeline Delmore leaned close and lowered her voice as she helped herself to another orange-frosted cookie. "Are they really *amazing* in bed after they've zapped a ghost? I've heard the sex is unbelievable right after a burn."

The question caught Virginia Burch just as she took a sip of the sparkling wine punch. She coughed and sputtered. Heat infused her cheeks. Unfortunately, she reflected glumly, bright pink was not her best color, especially on her face. She glanced wildly around to make sure no one else had overheard Adeline's outrageous question.

The offices of Gage & Burch were crowded with friends and colleagues, some of whom she could not recognize because, even though they were here to celebrate her engagement, most wore masks and costumes. It was Halloween week, after all; otherwise known here in Cadence as party-till-you-drop week. She wondered if the fact that her friends had chosen to throw a surprise engagement party with a Halloween theme was a bad omen. Not that she needed any more to warn her that her forthcoming marriage was probably a huge mistake.

Luckily someone had cranked up the volume of the music. The throbbing beat of a rez-rock song created a blanket of white noise that effectively shrouded conversations. As far as she could tell, no one had overheard Adeline's question about the sexual habits of ghost-hunters.

"Uh," Virginia said. To buy herself some time, she groped for a napkin decorated with a cartoon picture of a woman in a pointy black hat and a cape, riding a broomstick. "Uh, well—"

"I've heard the stories," Adeline continued, eyes gleaming. "And if you'll recall, I dated that good-looking hunter for a while. The one with the blue eyes and the curly black hair. I can't remember his name."

"Brett." It was hard to keep up with Adeline's ever-changing list of boyfriends, Virginia thought. But Brett had been memorable mostly because he had been a swaggering braggart. Of course, a lot of ghost-hunters were swaggering braggarts.

But not Sam. Whatever else he was, he was not a typical hunter.

She glanced across the room to where her new combination fiancé/business partner stood talking with one of the guests. Sam Gage didn't have to do any bragging, she thought wistfully. You knew just by looking at him that he could take care of himself and any ghost that happened along.

She was pretty sure he'd be terrific in bed, too, but she was beginning to think she might never find out the truth of that for herself.

"Oh, yeah, right," Adeline said. "Brett. That was his name. At any rate, he made some very interesting claims and promises. Ghost-hunters are not exactly shy when it comes to telling you about their sexual prowess. But our relationship didn't last long enough for me to run an experiment. Anyhow, I'm curious. I realize it's none of my business—"

"No, it's not."

"But I *am* your very best friend in the entire world," Adeline reminded her. "If you can't tell me, who can you tell?"

Virginia cleared her throat and decided to be honest. "Sorry, I'm not in a position to answer your question."

Adeline looked dumbfounded. "You're not? But you're going to marry Sam Gage. He's a hunter. This is your engagement party."

"Oddly enough, it looks more like a Halloween party to me."

"Okay, okay, so we decided to give it a theme. All the best parties have themes. I read it in last month's issue of *Harmonic Home & Garden*."

"I can't believe *Harmonic Home & Garden* told you that Halloween is considered an appropriate theme for an engagement party."

"Personally, I thought it was kind of original." Adeline looked across the crowded room to where Sam stood. A speculative light glittered in her deceptively innocent eyes. "Are you telling me that you two haven't done it yet? How weird."

"Adeline, I explained that Sam and I intend to apply for a two-year marriage-of-convenience license, not a covenant license."

"So what? That doesn't mean you aren't going to sleep together, does it?" Adeline broke off abruptly, eyes widening. *"Does it?"*

"This is business." Virginia swallowed. "I told you that."

Adeline looked skeptical. "One hundred percent business?"

"Yes."

"No fooling around at all?"

Virginia fought to quell the panic that had been nibbling at her for the past few days. "Like I said, it's a business arrangement."

Adeline groaned. "I don't believe it. You and Sam are a perfect couple."

Virginia paused, her plastic cup of punch halfway to her mouth. "What ever gave you that idea?"

"Are you kidding? You and Sam were made for each other. You've got so much in common."

"Such as?"

Adeline's brow climbed. "Well, for openers, you're both repressed, obsessive workaholics. Neither one of you seems to know how to have fun."

"Thanks a lot."

Adeline chuckled. "Should have seen the looks on your faces when you walked into the office this evening."

"We weren't expecting a party, Adeline."

"Yeah, I know." Adeline smiled smugly. "It was a surprise party. And it worked, didn't it?"

Virginia thought about the way her stomach had clenched when she had opened the door a short time earlier and been greeted with shrieks of *"Surprise."*

"It worked," she mumbled into her punch. "I was definitely surprised."

Adeline gave her an admonishing frown. "A lot of people went to a lot of effort to pull this off. Do me a favor: Try to look like you're having a good time, okay? Sam is taking it in stride."

Sam could take anything in stride, Virginia thought morosely, even an unanticipated engagement party. She caught a glimpse of him through the forest of black and orange balloons that dangled from the ceiling. He was still talking to the earnest-looking man in glasses.

Even surrounded by bobbing cardboard goblins, plastic jack-o'-lanterns and several yards of black and orange crepe paper, he looked, as he invariably did, completely at ease, totally in control.

He was a powerful dissonance-energy para-resonator—a ghost-hunter—but, thankfully, he did not go in for the long-haired, supermacho, khaki-and-leather look favored by most hunters. Tonight he was dressed in a black T-shirt, black trousers, and a tan jacket that fit well across his broad shoulders. He wore his resonating amber in a simple, gold ring rather than set in a massive belt buckle or a flashy pendant.

There was a relaxed air about him. The graceful languor of a natural-born predator at ease between kills emanated from him in psychic waves. Virginia could feel the disturbing energy all the way across the room. No one else seemed to be particularly aware of that aura—both dangerous and deeply sensual—that enveloped him, but it stirred all the tiny hairs on the nape of her neck.

Another twinge of panic zapped through her, unsettling both her physical and paranormal senses. The combined assault on her awareness made her shiver. The anxiety attacks were getting worse, she thought. Every time she contemplated marriage to Sam, she felt the small, high-rez shocks of trepidation.

What had she done?

She had agreed to marry Sam Gage; that was what she had done. Granted, it was only a two-year marriage-of-convenience. Nevertheless, she was going to be legally tied to him for two full years.

What had she done?

She forced herself to take a couple of deep breaths. When that did not block the tide of uneasiness that was doing such strange things to her insides, she tried another sip of the wine punch.

Just a marriage-of-convenience. They were common enough. It would end in two years unless she and Sam elected to renew it for another two-year period. There would be no reason to do that, she assured herself; no excuse to convert the MC into a more formal and far more binding covenant marriage.

Adeline was right; she had to project a little more good-natured enthusiasm here, Virginia told herself. She had agreed to the MC, after all. It was a terrific business move. And she certainly could not blame her friends for throwing a party. They meant well. And she was genuinely fond of most of them.

She was surrounded with a representative sprinkling of the professional and not-so-professional types involved in the many legitimate and not-so-legitimate businesses that had grown up around the excavation of the Dead City of Old Cadence. There were a number of academics from the university who were in the process of building distinguished careers studying the alien ruins. There were also several contract and freelance para-archaeologists, such as herself, and a few of Sam's ghost-hunter buddies who provided security to the excavation teams. In addition, there was a colorful assortment of gallery owners, hustlers, and ruin rats who worked the fringes of the trade in alien artifacts.

It was a mixed lot, to say the least, but they were all bound by their mutual interest in making their livings from the exploration and excavation of the ruins left by the long-vanished Harmonics.

It should have been a cheerful occasion, but she could feel the panic nibbling at her stomach.

"Sorry, Adeline. I guess I'm not in a party mood tonight."

"Fake it," Adeline said with a stern look.

Virginia gave her a reluctant smile. "Yes, ma'am."

"That's better." Adeline searched her face more closely. "What's the matter? I thought you were excited about this arrangement. Why the cold feet?"

"I'm not getting cold feet."

"Yes, you are. This is your old pal, Adeline, remember? I

know you better than anyone else. You've been getting increasingly short-tempered and high-strung for the past two weeks."

Virginia glared at her and picked up the punch ladle. "I've been a little busy lately, okay? I just finished the Henderson job yesterday, and Sam and I signed our first joint client this morning. We start work on the project tomorrow. On top of everything else, my family is hassling me about this MC, even though I've explained a hundred times that it's just a business deal."

"Your family is still convinced that Sam is just taking advantage of you?"

"That's their official position." Virginia ladled more punch into her cup. "But the truth is, they want me to settle down in a covenant marriage with Duncan."

Adeline shrugged. "Can't blame them. Duncan is a great catch. Good family, good connections. Nice guy."

"Duncan and I are friends, but it will never amount to more than that." Virginia dropped the ladle back into the bowl and took a hefty swallow of the punch. "Duncan and I both know it, even if our families don't."

"You mean you don't love him, and he doesn't love you."

"Yes. That's exactly what I mean."

Adeline raised her brows. "So, instead of a nice, safe marriage to good ol' Duncan, you're going to take a flyer on a two-year MC with a man you hardly know and who is a ghost-hunter to boot. Gee, can't imagine why the family is upset about that decision. Nope. Can't think of a single reason why your relatives would have a problem with your plans."

Virginia gave her a speaking glance. "It's business."

Adeline assumed an infuriating all-knowing expression. "Know what I think?"

"What?"

"I think you've got a radical case of nerves. Bridal jitters, as my aunt Sally would say."

"That's ridiculous. Why would I be nervous?"

"Excellent question."

"This is just a business deal." Virginia suspected that she was beginning to sound desperate. She tried to temper her tone. She wanted to sound calm and cool. As calm and cool as Sam had sounded when he had presented her with the proposition three weeks ago.

"This section of the Old Quarter is slated for gentrification within the next couple of years," he had explained. "Investors and developers are already starting to nose around. This house is going to be worth a fortune soon. But in the meantime, I've got to find a way to hang on to it."

She gazed at her new landlord in genuine alarm. She had rented her office and her upstairs apartment from him less than two months ago. She had found the old house at the end of a long, fruitless day spent tracking down the addresses of virtually every affordable rental in the Old Quarter of Cadence City. It had not been an advertised rental, but she had decided to make inquiries after noting the small sign on the door, which read Dead City Security, Sam Gage, Prop.

Her intent had been to ask the unknown Mr. Gage, who was clearly a small businessperson like herself, if he was aware of any suitable space in the neighborhood. The choicest rentals, she had learned, were frequently obtained by word of mouth rather than through the want ads.

Her initial impression of Sam Gage, the owner and sole employee of Dead City Security, was that he was not what one expected in a ghost-hunter who had set up shop as a security consultant. She had found him in his office, ankles propped on his desk, deep into the current issue of the *Journal of Para-Archaeology*. Heavy reading for a ghost-hunter, she thought. Most of the ones she knew preferred *Sex-Starved Psychic Playmates* and *Naked Amazon Maidens of the Alien Catacombs*.

Before the end of the conversation, Gage had offered her

an office on the first floor and an apartment on the second. She had fallen in love with both spaces the moment she had seen them. She was beginning to think that she had fallen in love with her new landlord at approximately the same time, but that was another issue altogether, one she did not want to confront.

"Hang on to it?" she repeated warily. "Is there a problem?"

"Just the usual. Taxes, upkeep, repairs." He spread the fingers of his amber-ringed hand in a gesture that encompassed all the trials and tribulations of home ownership. "This house was built right after the Era of Discord. That makes it over a hundred and fifty years old. It was built to last, so it's sound, but it needs a lot of work."

"I see." She looked around at the elegant molding, gleaming wooden floors, and uniquely framed windows.

The place was perfect for her one-person consulting business. The location, only two short blocks from the great, green quartz wall that surrounded the Dead City, was ideal. Her work required frequent trips both above ground and deep into the catacombs of the ancient alien ruins. From here, she could walk to her job site, which meant she would not have the expense of a car.

She cleared her throat uneasily. "Are you thinking of raising the rent already? Because, if so, I'd like to remind you that I do have a one-year lease."

He braced his hands on the top of her desk and leaned slightly forward. His amber-colored eyes were steady and intent. "No, I'm not going to raise your rent. I've got a proposition for you. If things work out the way I think they will, we'll both make a killing."

His idea had been a straightforward business arrangement. A marriage-of-convenience and a merger of her consulting business with his Dead City Security. He'd painted a dazzling picture. Operating as a single entity, Gage & Burch Consulting, they would double their resources overnight. Together, they would be able to compete for larger, more lucrative clients. The increased revenue would go into maintenance. The MC would ensure that they paid lower taxes. When the house was sold to developers in two years, they would share equally in the profits. A win-win situation.

All she had to do was find a way to be as cold-blooded about the arrangement as Sam. Unfortunately, the closer they drew to the date of the wedding, the less certain she was that such a thing was possible.

"I told you," Virginia said to Adeline. "Sam wants to hang on to this house until some developer is willing to pay big bucks for it. He offered to cut me in on the profits. It's a terrific business opportunity for me." Who was she trying to convince? She wondered.

Adeline reached for a piece of neon-orange candy. "Maybe the fact that it's just a business deal is part of the problem. Maybe that's not what you want."

No, Virginia thought. It most definitely was not what she wanted. Late this afternoon, after a long walk and a cup of coffee in the lonely little park at the end of the street, she had finally forced herself to face that fact. She was in love with Sam, but all he wanted from her was her signature on a contract. Marriage, especially a marriage-of-convenience, would be hell. The frustration factor alone would probably drive her to the nearest para-psych ward within a month. She was almost sure now that she could not go through with the arrangement.

But she had not yet figured out how to tell Sam.

She had planned to get things out in the open tonight. Then she had opened the door of the office and walked straight into the engagement party.

She could hardly bring up the subject now in the midst of a party. She would wait until morning. Tomorrow would be soon enough to tell him that she was having second thoughts.

She felt a guilty sense of relief at having made the decision to put off the inevitable for another few hours.

She was getting cold feet. He could feel the chill clear across the room. Every time he caught her eye, she averted her gaze or started up an earnest conversation with whoever happened to be standing nearby.

The last of the guests finally departed shortly after midnight. Sam closed the door behind the laggard and turned to see Virginia sinking down into the chair behind her desk. His bride-to-be looked both relieved and exhausted. She also looked cross. But then, lately she frequently looked tense and irritable. Bridal jitters. The odd thing was that the more anxious she got, the calmer and more certain he became.

She leaned back in the chair and closed her eyes. "Thought they'd never go."

"They meant well," he said.

"I know." She rested her head against the back of her chair. "But they don't understand."

"Sure they do. We're getting married. People like to celebrate marriages. Even MCs."

"I don't see why."

"Because there is a streak of the romantic buried somewhere inside most people," he explained patiently. "Deep down, everyone hopes that marriages-of-convenience will morph into the real thing."

"That's a highly unrealistic expectation. Statistically speaking, most MCs end on the first or second renewal date unless someone makes a mistake and gets pregnant." She paused meaningfully. "And there is absolutely no excuse for that kind of mistake."

"Right. No excuse."

Few mistakes of that sort were made because the First Generation colonists who had settled Harmony had crafted very strict legislation covering marriage and family. The more lib-

eral social policies of Earth had been abandoned when the
energy Curtain that had served as a gate between worlds had
unexpectedly closed, stranding the settlers. The founders, desperate to provide a social structure that would ensure the sur-
vival of the colony, had opted for stern laws. But in their
wisdom, the First Generation planners had also understood that
harsh rules that did not take human weaknesses into account
would ultimately fail. Failure of the social structure of the tiny
band of desperate settlers would mean catastrophe.

In an effort to deal with basic human foibles, the founders
had provided the socially and legally sanctioned marriages-of-
convenience to cover many of the traditional and less-than-
romantic reasons that drove people into wedlock: family
pressure, business, or simple passion. Couples who elected to
have children were expected to file for the more formal covenant marriage.

The muted warble and twang of a high-rez rock guitar
sounded from the street. Sam crossed the office to the window,
made a space between the blinds, and studied the night-
shrouded sidewalk.

The Old Quarter teemed with revelers tonight. The heavy
river fog that had cloaked Cadence nightly for the past several
days had deterred no one. People dressed as witches, goblins,
and ghosts—the fairytale sort, not the very real remnants of
dangerous alien energy known as *unstable dissonance energy
manifestations*—drifted in and out of the mists. Orange lights
came and went eerily in the shadows. As Sam watched, a
grinning jack-o'-lantern appeared out the gloom. Someone
shrieked in pretended fright. Raucous laughter echoed in the
night.

This was Halloween eve, and the noise level was already
high. Tomorrow night, Halloween night, would be bedlam.
Half of Cadence would flock to the Old Quarter to party. There
was no place in town quite as atmospheric at Halloween as

the seedy districts adjacent to the ancient walls of the Dead City.

In this part of town, ambient psi energy leaked continuously through tiny, often invisible cracks in the emerald-colored stones. It seeped up from the endless miles of green quartz tunnels and corridors beneath the pavement. The little currents and eddies of energy were part of the lure of the Old Quarters of all the cities on Harmony that had been built near the sites of ancient ruins. Tourists and locals alike loved the creepy sensations, especially at this time of year.

Maybe there was something to the theory that the flickers of psychic and para energy were stronger at this time of year, Sam thought. Ever since he had been a kid running loose on the streets, it had always seemed to him that he was more aware of the traces of ancient alien psi energy at Halloween. Tonight was no exception. The not-quite-human trickles of power that leaked out of the Dead City felt very strong. The stuff whispered through his mind, making him deeply aware of the unseen paranormal world that hovered just beyond the range of the physical senses. The surge in power levels that he detected were probably nothing more than the result of his overactive imagination, he thought. The same imagination that had conjured up the brilliant idea of talking Virginia into a marriage-of-convenience.

In hindsight, all he could say was that it had seemed like a good idea at the time.

Behind him, Virginia yawned. "We'd better get some sleep. Mac Ewert will be expecting us early tomorrow morning. He's anxious to get his excavation site cleared so that he can get his team back on the job. He made a big point of reminding me of how much money he's losing with every day of lost work."

"You're right. We need some sleep. Don't want to doze off in front of Gage & Burch's first client." Sam turned away from the window. "I'll see you to your door."

For a few seconds, the tension in her eyes retreated. She gave him a familiar, laughing smile, the kind of smile she had bestowed on him frequently until he had asked her to merge her business with his and file for an MC. At the sight of the glowing look, he felt his whole body tighten. The desire he had worked so hard to conceal for the past two months heated his blood. With every passing hour it was getting harder to quash the rush of sexual anticipation that stirred him whenever he was near Virginia.

By the time his nonwedding night arrived, he would be a basket case.

What the *hell* had he been thinking? A marriage-of-convenience in which he slept on the third floor while Virginia slept on the second floor was going to make him certifiably crazy.

She rose from the chair and stretched. "I thought it was my turn to see you to your door."

"Want to flip a coin?"

"Okay, but this time let's try one of my mine. I don't trust that one that you like to use. It always comes up heads." She dug a quarter out of her pocket. "Call it."

"Heads." He moved toward her.

She flipped the coin into the air. He caught it before it struck the polished surface of her desk.

"Heads," he said without bothering to look at it.

She wrinkled her nose. "You're in luck. I'm too tired to argue."

At the door of the office, she paused to switch off the lights. He followed her out into the front hall and locked up. Together, they climbed the elaborately carved central staircase to the second floor and went down the corridor to the small suite of rooms she used as an apartment.

She opened her door, stepped inside, and swung around to face him through the narrow opening. Her green-and-gold eyes were big and deep in the shadows. He could feel the tingle of awareness in his paranormal senses and knew that he was responding to her on the psychic plane as well as on the physical level. Sensual psi energy shimmered disturbingly in the small space that separated them. Couldn't she sense it? He wondered. Was she really oblivious to the attraction between them?

The wariness in her eyes made him uneasy. With each passing day, she appeared to be growing more restless. His fears of being driven crazy by sexual frustration were submerged beneath a new concern: What if she changed her mind? What if she canceled the MC?

Stay focused, he told himself. *This will work.* It had to work.

"Good night," he said as casually as he could manage. He forced himself to take a step back. What he really wanted to do was pick her up and carry her through the small living room, straight into her bedroom. "I'll see you in the morning."

She hesitated. "Sam?"

"Yeah?" He realized that he had stopped breathing.

She sighed. "Never mind. It's not important. Good night."

Very gently, she closed the door in his face.

He reminded himself to breathe.

Two

He did not sleep well that night. It was not the noise from the crowds in the street or the whispers of Dead City psi energy that kept him awake. It was the realization that Virginia was getting ready to tell him that she did not want to go through with the marriage. He knew it as surely as he knew that when she called off the engagement, his world was going to become as bleak and gray as the tide of fog that had boiled up out of the river.

He rolled out of bed at dawn, shaved, showered, and dressed for the meeting with Ewert. He was still mulling over various means of convincing Virginia that the MC was a terrific idea when he went downstairs to collect the morning edition of the *Cadence Star*. He opened the front door and was greeted by a wall of gray mist. The fog was so thick that it had blotted out the early-morning sun, creating an artificial twilight that looked as if it would last all day.

Perfect Halloween weather.

He shrugged off the fog. It would not affect today's job. He and Virginia would be working underground in the catacombs. Down below in the endless miles of glowing green corridors, there was no day or night.

He saw the small package on the step just as he started to reach for the newspaper. A faint hiss of all-too-familiar psi energy whispered through his para senses in silent warning.

"Damn." Hell of a way to start the day.

He crouched on his heels to get a closer look at the square object wrapped in brown paper. It was addressed to Gage & Burch Consulting. There was no return address. He did not pick it up.

"Something wrong, Sam?" Virginia called out from half-way down the stairs.

"An unscheduled delivery." He did not take his eyes off the package.

"What is it?"

"I think you'd better take a look at this. If I'm right, it falls into your area of expertise, not mine."

She descended the rest of the stairs quickly and hurried across the wide front hall to the door. She came to a halt beside him and looked at the package.

She pursed her lips thoughtfully. "Uh-oh."

"I hate it when you use that professional jargon." He glanced at her. "What do you think?"

"The same thing you're thinking, I imagine. It's an illusion trap. I can feel the energy pattern. Someone left us a nasty little trick. I'll bet it was some idiot who had one too many bottles of Green Ruin to drink last night. Probably thought it would be a great Halloween prank."

"I think he'll change his mind when I find him," Sam said softly.

Virginia glanced at him, frowning slightly. "Don't worry, it's just a small trap."

"Can you de-rez it?"

"Does amber resonate? Of course I can de-rez it. But I'm

not going to do it out here on the front step. Let's take it into the kitchen.''

She reached down and scooped up the box with a nonchalance that made Sam wince. He followed her into the big kitchen at the back of the house and watched her set the box down on the scarred counter.

''You might want to stand back a little,'' she said as she clipped the string. ''Just in case.''

''We're partners, remember?'' He moved closer to the counter.

She smiled as she began to unwrap the package. ''Yes, but you've never seen me work. I wouldn't blame you for being a tad cautious. Even small, simple illusion traps can be very unpleasant if they aren't untangled properly.''

''I've spent a lot of time underground and I've worked with some clumsy tanglers. I've caught the flashback from an accidentally sprung trap more than once.''

''Well, there won't be any flashback this time. You have my personal guarantee.''

Her cool, professional arrogance amused him. He watched her peel away the brown paper. A small cardboard box was revealed. With a good deal more caution than she had exercised a moment ago, she raised the lid and gazed inside.

''Well, well, well,'' she murmured. She sounded as cheerful as if she had just received a bouquet of flowers.

Personally, he could think of a number of other things he would rather find on his doorstep first thing in the morning besides an illusion trap. But if the challenge of de-rezzing it lifted Virginia's spirits and gave her something else to think about besides calling off their marriage, he might be willing to overlook the prank.

''What is it?'' he asked.

''A very nice piece.'' She angled the box to allow him a closer look at the object inside. ''A little unguent jar. Museum quality. Not spectacular, but quite excellent. It would bring a good price in a gallery. I can't imagine anyone in his right mind wasting it just to play a vicious Halloween trick.''

Sam eyed the small green quartz jar. It was elegantly rounded in a shape that was not quite comfortable for a human hand. The top was carved in an airy, fanciful design similar to many he had seen in the course of his career. The art and sculpture left behind by the long-vanished Harmonics always reminded him of the Old Earth poet Goethe's description of architecture: *frozen music*.

"You're right," he said. "It's not unique, but it's definitely valuable. Whoever our prankster is, he must be a wealthy collector if he could afford to use an artifact worth a couple of grand just to pull off a Halloween stunt."

An illusion trap had to be anchored to an artifact or to old green quartz from the ruins.

"Probably too drunk to realize what he was doing." Virginia carefully lifted the top of the jar and peered into the dark interior. "Okay, here we go. It's a simple pattern. This won't take long."

"Easy for you to say." He looked down into the shadows inside the little unguent jar. The darkness there was not normal. There was a dense quality to it, the only visible warning of the tiny trap. In the eerie glow of the green catacombs of the Dead City it was all too easy for a member of an excavation team to mistake illusion dark for ordinary shadow, but here in the brightly lit kitchen, the difference was obvious to the trained eye.

Obvious, but no less dangerous.

He had seen other tanglers work, but this was the first time he had watched Virginia in action. She'd only had a handful of clients during the time she had been renting office space from him, and she had dealt with them on her own.

He felt psi energy spark and shiver in the air. Very highrez. He was impressed. She was as powerful as her academic credentials claimed.

Technically speaking, she was an ephemeral-energy para-resonator; a tangler in common parlance. With the aid of the specially tuned amber that she wore in her earrings, she could focus her particular type of paranormal energy in a way that allowed her to neutralize the vicious and sometimes deadly illusion traps. The wicked snares were one of the hazards of para-archaeological work in the alien ruins. The vast majority of tanglers became para-archaeologists. It was one of two natural career paths, the second being the illegal antiquities market.

An illusion trap was tricky. Once tripped, it released a web of ephemeral psi energy in an alien nightmare that enveloped the mind of the unlucky person who had triggered it. No two traps produced the same harrowing visions. Some were simple to de-rez, especially the really old ones. But in later Harmonic traps, the energy had been woven into complex patterns that defied all but the most skilled tanglers.

No one who had ever survived the experience of being caught in an illusion trap's web could ever fully describe the nightmares. Sam had sensed enough on the occasions when he had been zapped with some of the flashback energy from a poorly sprung trap to know that the visions were composed of unimaginable colors and a vertigo-inspiring darkness. The experts claimed that the nightmares lasted only a few minutes before the human brain sought refuge in unconsciousness. The resulting coma, however, could last for hours or days. When the victim eventually awakened, he or she invariably suffered an amnesia that cloaked most memories of the event. Some never recovered completely. They tended to end up in the para-psych wards of mental institutions. Others were so traumatized they could never work underground again.

No one knew why the Harmonics had booby trapped their underground catacombs. Whoever their enemies had been, they were as long gone as those who had set snares for them.

"Got it," Virginia said with soft satisfaction. She took a

breath and looked up from the jar. "Didn't even heat up my amber. It's clean."

"Nice job." He picked up the jar and turned it in his hands, examining it from every angle. The fizz of malign energy that had warned him of the trap had ceased. The trap could be reset by a skilled tangler, but unless that was done, the unguent jar was safe to handle.

He looked down into the interior. The unnatural, viscous shadow was gone. In its place was the ordinary darkness one expected to find in the interior of any small vessel. There was also something else inside the little jar. He pulled out a square of folded paper.

Virginia frowned. "It looks like a note."

"Yes, it does, doesn't it? Maybe our prankster wants to brag. Thoughtful of him to provide a clue." He unfolded the paper and read aloud the single sentence typed on it. " 'Happy Halloween. The ghosts and goblins are real in the catacombs this week. Stay out. This will be your only warning.' "

"What in the world?"

"Not real original," Sam remarked.

Virginia snatched the paper from his hand. "Let me see that." Her brows drew together in a stern line as she read it silently. Then she looked at him. "What do you think this is all about?"

"I think," Sam said, "that one of Mac Ewert's competitors doesn't want us to go to work for him. Wouldn't be the first time a rival has tried to scare off another team's consultants."

"Huh." She dropped the note into the trash. "Obviously whoever sent this doesn't realize who they're dealing with. The firm of Gage & Burch doesn't get scared off *that* easily."

Sam saw the gutsy determination in her eyes and smiled. For some reason he suddenly felt a lot more optimistic about his marriage prospects than he had when he had come downstairs earlier.

•   •   •

"Damndest thing I've ever seen." Mac Ewert ran a blunt-fingered hand through his thinning gray hair. "I've heard of waterfalls, but I've been mapping catacombs for twenty years, and this is the first one I've ever run into."

"They're rare," Sam agreed. "But I think we can handle it for you."

Virginia felt her jaw drop. She barely managed to conceal her shock. She was amazed by Sam's casual response to Ewert's announcement. They were going to have to de-rez a *waterfall?* She almost groaned aloud. Of all the bad luck. This was just what they did not need for their first time out as the new firm of Gage & Burch; a nearly impossible assignment. She was the one who had taken the call yesterday morning from Mac. He had certainly not mentioned anything about a waterfall.

She reminded herself that waterfalls fell into Sam's area of expertise. She had to admire him for projecting an image of professional confidence, but she seriously doubted that he'd had any experience with waterfalls. Few people had.

She had read about them, of course. They were described in the textbooks as unique cascades of unstable dissonance-energy manifestations—ghosts—that could block entire corridors. Unlike most UDEMs, they did not drift aimlessly through the underground tunnels of the Dead City. Instead, they were anchored in one place, forming impenetrable walls of seething psi energy that could fry anyone dumb enough to get too close. Little was known about them because so few had been discovered. Those that had been found had been de-rezzed by teams of very expensive, highly specialized experts, not by small-time security consultants. Sam would be on his own with this one. Her name was now on the newly repainted door of the office, but that didn't mean she could help him with the waterfall. This was a job for a ghost-hunter. A really, really good ghost-hunter. All she could do was cheer him on.

Ewert gave Sam a look of mingled desperation and aggressive demand. "Think you can handle it, Gage? This project is already running behind schedule. I've had one delay after another in the tunnels during the past month. I can't afford any more."

"I'll take a look," Sam said. "I can give you a firm answer as soon as I examine it."

Ewert planted his hands on his desk and glanced at the khaki-and-leather clad man who lounged against the wall. "Leon, here, doesn't think any single hunter can deactivate it. He tells me I'm going to have to contract with the guild for a team of specialists. Trouble is, my budget won't stretch that far."

"It's big," Leon drawled. "More ghost energy than I've ever seen in one place and I've been working underground for damn near fifteen years."

Virginia glanced at him. Leon Drummond was the Ewert team's ghost-hunter. He was working on a standard guild contract. He had made it clear that he resented having a private consultant brought in to handle the waterfall problem.

Leon was everything that gave ghost-hunters a bad name, as far as Virginia was concerned. He was arrogant, macho, ill-mannered, and he had poor taste in clothes. His oversized belt buckle was studded with so much amber that if he ever fell into the river, she was pretty sure that he would sink like a stone.

"Like I said, I can give you an answer after I've had a look at the waterfall," Sam said calmly.

"Suit yourself," Leon muttered.

Ewert leaned wearily back in his chair. "Leon will take you to the site. I can't allow anyone else into that corridor until the waterfall is cleared. Too dangerous. For God's sake, don't do anything stupid. If you and Miss Burch can't handle it, just say so. My insurance won't cover any lawsuits."

Sam nodded as he got to his feet. "We'll keep that in mind. Ready, Virginia?"

If nothing else, this was going to be interesting, she thought. Not many people got an opportunity to see a real ghost-energy waterfall. In spite of her misgivings, anticipation rose within her.

"Ready," she said.

With a shrug, Leon managed to straighten himself away from the office wall. He turned and sauntered out through the door without a word. Sam and Virginia followed him outside to where the utility vehicle waited.

The eerie green glow given off by the emerald-hued quartz that lined the alien catacombs always had the same effect on Virginia: It sent a tiny chill of dread and wonder down her spine. The sensation was not a thrill of fear exactly; more a deep, elemental response to that which was not human. She had grown up in the very shadow of the ancient ruins, and she had been aware of her own psychic response to the peculiar energy that resonated within its walls since childhood. But she did not think that she would ever be entirely comfortable in the mysterious tunnels. Some part of her would always feel like an intruder here.

No one knew what the ancient Harmonics had looked like. No pictures or records of physical descriptions had ever been found. None of the art that had survived depicted the vanished beings who had created it. No one could even guess why Harmony's original inhabitants had built these endless miles of catacombs, most of which had never been charted. But one thing was certain: The business of exploring, mapping, and excavating relics from the ruins was big. And the competition could be fierce.

Virginia sat next to Sam on the second bench of the small, open-sided utility truck. Leon Drummond took the wheel, piloting the vehicle through the maze of intersecting corridors with the aid of an amber-rez locator. He had remained sullenly silent since leaving Ewert's office.

Sam had not had much to say, either. Virginia studied him out of the corner of her eye. He was playing it cool, she thought. But, then, Sam always played it cool. If he had any doubts about confronting a dangerous waterfall of unstable dissonant energy, he did not allow them to show.

Virginia wanted to ask him why he had not mentioned the illusion trap they had found on their doorstep that morning to Mac Ewert, but she was not about to bring up the subject in front of Leon Drummond.

There was another, more personal matter that she had not yet gotten around to this morning, either, she reminded herself: marriage. She had promised herself that she would tell Sam about her growing doubts, but then had come the business of the illusion trap, and after that they'd had to hurry in order to make the meeting with Ewert.

What with one thing and another, she had found excuses not to deal with the issue of their marriage.

She glanced at the glowing green maw of an intersecting corridor as Leon drove past. There was a warning sign posted at the entrance. Keep Out. Unmapped Zone. Sort of like her engagement, she thought. Another little chill went through her, but this time it had nothing to do with the alien catacombs. She would talk to Sam this evening, she promised herself. Right after they had finished this consulting project.

She could not put it off another day. Her nerves couldn't take the stress.

She studied the quartz walls as the utility truck traveled along the corridor. The endless green stone passages were interrupted here and there by small, slightly less than human-sized openings that, she knew from experience, led to chambers. Most of the rooms and anterooms discovered in the underground regions of the ancient city were small, but some vast, exotic spaces had been found. Explorers had untrapped chambers so large and elegantly proportioned that many para-archaeologists assumed they had been used for ceremonial functions or royal tombs. But they could just as easily have been employed as underground aircraft hangers for all anyone knew.

Twenty minutes later, Leon slowed the cab and turned into the entrance of a branching tunnel. Virginia caught a glimpse of another warning sign. Keep Out: UDEM Ahead.

Leon brought the cab to a halt and finally deigned to speak. "The waterfall is down that corridor on the right."

The announcement was unnecessary. The pulsing, acid-green light of the unnaturally large concentration of ghost energy was already visible. It throbbed at the entrance of the corridor. Virginia gazed at it, amazed. She had never seen that much ghost light in one place in her entire career. She could only guess at the size of the UDEM itself. It was still out of sight around the corner.

Beside her, Sam moved. He got out of the cab and walked toward the entrance of the branching corridor. His hard face was etched in lines of concentration and keen anticipation. He was looking forward to this, Virginia thought. Well, what else had she expected? He was a ghost-hunter, after all, and this was undoubtedly the most dangerous, most challenging energy specter he had ever been called upon to de-rez. She would probably be feeling the same excitement if they were confronting a particularly complex illusion trap.

Sam paused at the entrance of the tunnel. He glanced back at her over his shoulder "Wait here. I'm going to take a closer look."

Leon draped his arms on the steering wheel and watched Sam disappear around the corner into the pulsing green light. "This won't take long. Once he sees the size of that thing, he'll be back. He'd have to be a fool to try to tackle that sucker on his own."

Virginia did not like his tone. The last thing she wanted to do was wait here with Leon.

"I'm going with him." She hopped lightly down from the truck.

Leon scowled. "Are you a hunter, too?"

"No, I'm a tangler."

"This ain't no job for a tangler," Leon said. "That's a ghost in there, not some wimpy little illusion trap."

Virginia ignored him. She went quickly toward the tunnel entrance. When she rounded the corner, she was nearly blinded by the fierce, oddly cold glare. She narrowed her eyes against the intense glow and saw Sam. He was silhouetted in front of a cascading wall of pure green energy: the waterfall.

It was an astonishing sight. Light tumbled, swirled, and flowed in oceanlike waves that poured in an endlessly circulating fountain from ceiling to floor and back again. The wall of churning energy blocked the entire corridor, which was narrower than most. The interior dimensions were much smaller than those of the outer tunnel where Leon Drummond waited in the truck.

For some reason, the silence of the waterfall struck Virginia as strange, even though she had seen enough ghosts in her time to know that there was rarely much noise associated with them. A few pops and crackles and the occasional hiss of the ice-cold energy constituted the usual range of the sound effects.

"It really does look like a waterfall," she exclaimed as she went forward to join Sam. "You'd almost expect to see a river or a pool of psi energy forming at the bottom."

Sam frowned at her. "I thought I told you to wait in the truck."

"Not a chance." She gazed at the tumbling green waves. "We're a team, remember?"

"This isn't illusion energy."

"Right. You're the expert on this stuff. I'll just supervise."

He hesitated. "I've always worked alone."

"Not anymore." She turned toward him. "It was your idea to merge our businesses, remember?"

He gave her an odd look. "Yeah. I remember."

She turned back to the cascades of green fire. "Well? What's your professional opinion, Mr. Ghost-Hunter? Can you handle it?"

Sam did not answer immediately, but his eyes gleamed in the reflected glow. His mouth curved slightly.

"Does amber resonate?" he asked with just a hint of old-fashioned ghost-hunter arrogance. "Yeah, I can handle it. But I'll have to de-rezz it one section at a time."

"Why?"

"Because it's not really one large ghost. It's composed of a number of smaller UDEMs that have been linked to create the waterfall effect."

"Aha. That makes sense. Whoever did this also figured out how to anchor it in place, too, like an illusion trap. I've never heard of a ghost that didn't just drift aimlessly."

Sam moved a little closer to the waterfall. "It's old. Very, very old. Probably been here for eons."

"I can believe it." Virginia shivered. "I'm sure the ancients knew a lot of Halloween tricks that we humans will uncover the hard way."

"Might as well get to work." Sam walked slowly across the width of the tunnel, as though measuring the breadth of the waterfall. He came to a halt at one side.

Virginia felt the invisible rush of human psi energy. A lot of it. She had seen Sam work before but never on a project that demanded so much para-talent. She took a respectful step back, not wanting to get in his way or disturb his concentration. De-rezzing this monster ghost was going to take a great deal of focused psi power.

Silence hummed for a few minutes.

Waterfall light flared, glinting off Sam's strong cheekbones. The green glare transformed the hard planes and angles of his face into an eerie, menacing mask. He gazed, seemingly riveted by the waterfall.

It was probably because he was concentrating so intently on the job at hand that she was the one who heard the high-pitched whine of the utility truck's engine first. She glanced back over her shoulder, surprised to see that Leon had braved the corridor, after all.

The small truck barreled toward where she stood with Sam in front of the waterfall. It was moving quickly; too quickly. She put up a hand to warn Leon to halt.

Then she realized that Leon was not at the wheel. No one was in the open-sided truck. Someone had rezzed the engine, slammed it into gear, and sent it hurtling down the narrow corridor toward Sam and her. It was a tight fit. Assuming the vehicle continued to travel in a straight line, there would be only a foot of clearance on either side. With a sickening sensation in the pit of her stomach, she realized that even if they could flatten themselves into that small space, it would do them no good. When the truck slammed into the energy waterfall, there would be an explosion. The flashback of ghost energy would crash over them. If they survived the experience, the tide of raw alien energy would fry their brains. She and Sam would not be able to do much more than sit in front of a rez-screen watching sitcoms twenty-four hours a day for the rest of their lives.

If they survived. And that was a very big if.

"Sam."

He swung around, taking in the situation in a single glance.

"Sonofabitch." He scooped her up in his arms. "Hang on. Tight."

She wanted to argue, but there didn't seem to be much point. There was no place to run. She wrapped her arms around his neck and buried her face against his chest, filling her senses with the scent of him one last time. If they were going to go, she couldn't think of anyone she would rather go with than Sam.

"I love you," she whispered into his shirt.

But she knew that he had not heard her. For one thing, the utility truck was almost upon them now. The fully rezzed engine was screaming too loudly to make even normal levels of conversation possible.

The second thing that made a dramatic farewell impossible was that Sam was projecting an enormous amount of psi energy. She could feel it enveloping her as he held her tightly against his chest. So much power required the use of all of his internal resources, both physical and paranormal. The last thing he could do at that moment was pay attention to what she had muttered into his shirt. It was a wonder he had the strength to hold her in his arms.

She heard the whine of the swiftly advancing truck, felt Sam tighten his arms fiercely around her, and then, impossibly, she was suddenly aware of being surrounded by a rushing sea of alien energy. Ghost energy.

She realized that Sam had chosen to escape the utility truck by leaping through the waterfall with her in his arms.

The acid-green waterfall washed over her in a giant wave. She braced herself for the searing mind burn but, incredibly, the energy did not touch her. She could feel the weight of it pressing on her from all sides, sensed the raw power that seethed in the cascade, *but it did not touch her.* It was as if she was protected by an invisible envelope.

The world whirled on its axis. She felt a jarring thud that took her breath. She heard Sam grunt and then she felt the cool green quartz beneath her. She realized that they had both landed on the floor of the corridor—on the other side of the waterfall.

Sam rolled with her in his arms, carrying her to the edge of the tunnel. They came up hard against the quartz wall.

Sam released her and got to his feet. He swung around to

face the cascade of green energy. Dazed, Virginia sat up slowly, pushing hair out of her eyes. She stared at the waterfall. Sam had carried her through that mass of alien energy. Without a scratch.

Unless, of course, this was how you felt after your brain got fried. Maybe her mind hadn't yet assimilated the fact of its own destruction. Perhaps a lifetime of sitcoms still awaited her. Heaven help her, maybe she would actually enjoy them.

Before she could mention that awful possibility to Sam, she heard the explosion on the other side of the UDEM waterfall. She knew what had happened because she had seen similar events, albeit on a far smaller scale. The utility truck had slammed into the energy wall and been bounced back like a rubber ball. The inevitable blast that accompanied the meeting of an immovable object and an unstoppable vehicle had taken place at the point of impact on the other side of the waterfall.

Here on the back side of the energy cascade, it was business as usual. There was no backwash of energy.

A stunning silence descended. Nothing broke it except the occasional hiss and crackle produced by the tumbling fountain of ghost energy.

"You did it." Virginia tore her gaze off the waterfall and looked at Sam. "You got us through it in one piece. How in the name of Old Earth did you manage it?"

"I didn't try to de-rez the whole damn waterfall. Just neutralized a section big enough to allow us to pass through for about thirty seconds." He spoke absently, as if his thoughts were on something else that was far more important. "Couldn't hold it any longer than that. At least not while I—" He broke off.

"You mean, you couldn't de-rez it for more than a few seconds and carry me through it at the same time," she said. "You don't have to spell it out. I know how much psi power that little leap through the waterfall must have cost you. I must have felt as heavy as that damn truck in your arms."

His brows rose. "A gentleman never calls attention to a lady's weight."

"I appreciate that." She frowned. "You must have melted your amber."

He glanced at his ring. "Yeah, it's fused. I've got a backup chunk, but I won't be able to use it for a while."

She looked around warily. The section of corridor in which they stood looked very much like the section on the other side of the waterfall. The same pale, luminous green glow infused the impermeable quartz. Here and there she caught the telltale trace of illusion shadow that marked the concealed door to a hidden room or antechamber. The dizzying maze of intersecting tunnels stretched out ahead as far as she could see.

The difference between this section of the catacombs and those on the other side of the waterfall, of course, was that this sector had not yet been officially mapped. The safest way out would be to go back through the waterfall, but that would not be possible until Sam had recovered from the aftereffects of melting amber. Besides, Leon Drummond might be waiting on the other side.

She checked her earrings. "My amber is still good. At least we won't lose our sense of direction."

Underground, the only thing that kept you oriented was tuned amber. Without it, the endless miles of eerie quartz tunnels became a hopelessly impenetrable labyrinth, even with a locator.

"Drummond tried to kill us," Sam said without inflection. "My guess is he's our Halloween trickster."

"The one who left that trap on our doorstep last night?"

"Yeah. Someone must be paying him very well to sabotage Ewert's map team. The guild frowns on that sort of thing. Bad public relations."

"Especially now when the guild is trying so hard to build a good public image." Virginia scrambled awkwardly to her feet. She glanced down, half-expecting to find scorch marks on her trousers. She saw nothing but a few new wrinkles. She looked up again. "Sam, you must be exhausted."

"Not yet. The afterburn is still kicking in. The buzz will last for about an hour. Then I'm going to have to crash for at least two or three hours. No way to beat it."

She nodded. The syndrome was well-known. Ghost-hunters who expended large amounts of psi energy needed time to recover.

Sam studied the corridors that branched off in different directions behind her. "We need to find a place where we can hole up for a while. In an hour I'm going to be asleep, like it or not."

She glanced around. "Why can't we just stay here? No one else is going to come through that waterfall."

"Probably not," Sam agreed. "But that's not what's got me worried."

"Well? What is worrying you? Aside from the fact that Drummond just tried to nail us?"

"It occurs to me that whoever hired Leon Drummond to keep Mac Ewert from making any progress in this corridor may be working illegally on *this* side of the waterfall."

Virginia widened her eyes as understanding hit her. "Yes, of course. An illegal excavation project on this side would explain a lot. But if you're right, we could run into Drummond's pals any minute."

"I'd say that's a definite risk." He started toward her. "Come on, we've got to find a place to hide until I can sleep off the afterburn."

"There are bound to be some chambers or rooms we can duck into for a few hours," she said. "All we have to do is pick one that doesn't look like it's been charted yet. Odds are no one will find us during the next few hours. Heck, I doubt if anyone will even come looking for us. Drummond must think we're dead. He'll no doubt report that we got reckless, got ourselves fried by that waterfall, and that the firm of Gage & Burch is out of business.''

"True. He can't have any way of knowing that we survived. All the same, I don't want to take any more chances than necessary." Sam looked at her. "We haven't got a lot of time."

The prowling urgency in him worried her. She opened her mouth to say something reassuring, but the words got caught in her throat. He was only a short distance away now. For the first time since they had come through the waterfall, she got a close look at his eyes. What she saw there stilled her breath for a few seconds.

Hot, intense, brilliant; sexual desire, elemental and dangerously compelling, blazed in his eyes. His gaze literally glittered with what, in any other circumstances, she might have mistaken for the first evidence that he felt a degree of genuine passion for her.

Adeline's question came back to her in an uncomfortable rush. *"So, is it true what they say about ghost-hunters? Are they really amazing in bed after they've zapped a ghost? I've heard the sex is unbelievable right after a burn."*

What she saw in Sam now, she realized, was no more than the aftereffects of a massive expenditure of ghost-hunter psi talent. Chemically speaking, it was the result of a combination of testosterone, adrenaline, and the potent biological cocktail his paranormal powers had dumped into his bloodstream.

Nothing personal, she reminded herself. He wasn't attracted to her, per se. It just happened that he was rezzed for sex, and she was the only female in sight. Anything in skirts would probably do just fine for him at that moment.

"Uh, Sam? Are you okay?"

"No." He went past her, heading for the first branching corridor. "Let's get moving."

Three

He was freaking her out. He knew it, but there wasn't much he could do about it. Hanging on to his self-control required every shred of what little willpower he could muster. Getting them both safely through the waterfall had required more power than he'd ever used in his life; more than he'd known he possessed. He did not intend to tell Virginia the truth: that it had been damned close. They had made it, but in the process he'd poured so much psychic wattage through his amber that he'd destroyed the resonating properties of the precision-tuned stone. Melting amber meant you'd pushed the envelope. There was always a price to pay.

He'd experienced the sexual buzz that often occurred after a major burn before. In the past, he'd always felt fully in control of the predictable arousal. But this time things were different. It wasn't just that the burn had been bigger; the real problem was that this time, he was alone with Virginia, the woman he'd been lusting after for nearly two months.

He was in the grip of a feverish desire that was all the worse because he had worked so hard to suppress and conceal it.

All right, so he had a major hard-on. Just a few rampaging hormones. So what? He wasn't a kid. He could control himself. He *had* to control himself. If he lost it now, he would probably terrify her and turn her against him forever. Any chance he had with her would go up in smoke.

He tried to concentrate on moving ahead down the corridor, searching the walls for the barest hint of illusion energy that would indicate a hidden chamber they could use. All of the rooms that had ever been discovered in the corridors had been found sealed with illusion traps. If they could find a sealed room that looked as if no one else had ever de-rezzed the trap that guarded it, Virginia could unseal it, and they could hide inside for a few hours.

Simple. All he had to do was concentrate and not think about the fact that she was only a few inches away.

"Sam, you're shivering." Virginia touched his forehead with gentle, questing fingers. "Good heavens, you're burning up. You must be running a temperature. Is this normal?"

"Damn it, *don't touch me.*" He closed his eyes briefly and drew a deep breath. Great. Now he was snapping at her. "We'll both be sorry if you do."

She frowned; not with fear or trepidation but with a concern that horrified him. If she started in with the sweet, nurturing stuff, he was doomed.

"This can't be normal," she insisted. "I think that burn must have made you ill."

"Trust me, it's normal," he said through set teeth. "A little intense, but normal."

He could not screw up and lose control. Not now. It was crucial that he did not scare her to death. Because maybe, just maybe, he really had heard her say "I love you" in those few seconds before he carried her through the waterfall.

"Slow down, Sam, I can't keep up with you."

He realized that he was loping down the corridor as he

raked the walls for telltale signs of illusion dark. "Sorry." He forced himself to slow somewhat.

"It's okay. Let me worry about finding a trapped chamber. We're back into my field of expertise now." She moved out ahead of him. "I think I see something up ahead. Yes, I can feel it."

He tried but he did not pick up the psychic tang of illusion dark. "I don't feel a damn thing."

"Probably because your para-senses are temporarily over-rezzed. But I'm sure there's something up there." She broke into a quick trot. "Positive. And it's big. A big trap usually indicates a large chamber. Maybe we'll luck out and find a palace. They always have lots of little antechambers around them. Plenty of places to hide."

He hoped she was right. Beneath the clawing surge of sexual need and the rush of the burn buzz, he thought he could detect the first warnings of the crash that would soon follow. He could not afford to collapse here in the open corridor. Not when there was a possibility that Leon Drummond's cohorts might be in the neighborhood. He had to stay on his feet long enough to make sure Virginia was safe.

He followed her around a bend and saw that she had come to a halt in front of what, at first glance, appeared to be a section of green quartz wall. But there was something not quite right about the center portion. He peered more closely, blinking to clear his jumpy vision. The wall wavered slightly before it came back into focus. Illusion dark.

"Big," he muttered.

"Yes. Very unusual. Also very, very old."

The thoughtful, decidedly academic tone of her voice worried him. The last thing they could afford to do was waste time while she analyzed the trap from a professional point of view.

"You can write it up for an article in the *Journal of Para-*

Archaeology when this is over," he said roughly. "Right now, we need to get into the space behind it."

She gave him a disgruntled look. "I know. Give me a minute here, though. There's something different about this trap."

A new wave of concern washed through him, rezzing up the already fizzing effects of the afterburn just as it had started to fade. "Can you handle it? Because if not, we've got to find another—"

"I can handle it," she assured him. "It's just . . . different, that's all. I can't explain—" She broke off. "Never mind."

She went to work untangling the trap that barred the door. Restlessly, he watched the corridor in both directions while she de-rezzed the entrance.

"Got it," Virginia whispered softly.

There was a disturbing note in her voice, but he did not have time to question her about it. He swung around and saw that there was now an opening in the green wall. Virginia had already moved through it.

He followed her quickly, surprised that he had to give his eyes a moment to adjust to the shadowy interior of the chamber. His first impression was of a vast space filled with green-drenched shadows. His surroundings glowed, just as the tunnel did, but the light emitted by the quartz was much weaker and much dimmer in here. The effect was an emerald twilight.

The only thing he could tell for certain was that this chamber was large, much bigger than any of the others he had ever seen. In the gloom he could not make out the far walls or the ceiling. The space was filled with a number of structures of various sizes, all fashioned of the familiar green quartz. They were packed closely together and piled on top of each other, forming what looked like miniature city blocks crammed with a number of small apartments. The blocks were separated by narrow, twisting lanes.

He started toward the nearest of the apartments, asssessing it as a potential hideout. He saw a narrow opening. It looked large enough to provide access to the interior of the building but small enough to be protected by a single man armed with a mag-rez gun.

Perfect.

"Hang on while I reset the trap," Virginia said behind him.

He paced restlessly while she worked. In a matter of seconds, illusion shadow once more obscured the entrance of the chamber.

"It won't deceive a trained tangler," she said as she turned back to face him, "but it might go unnoticed by a hunter or an excavation team worker, especially if he or she is in a hurry."

"With luck, there's no one out there looking for us."

"But you don't want to depend on luck, do you?"

"No." He scanned the dim chamber. "What the hell is this place?"

"Who knows?" She walked slowly toward him, searching the narrow canyons between the apartment-like structures. "I've never seen anything quite like it. Maybe it was a zoo. All those little cubicles and small rooms might have once been cages for animals."

"Maybe. Could just as easily have been a storage locker facility or an office park or a prison."

"We'll probably never know."

He came to a halt in front of the nearest apartment structure. It appeared to be several stories high. He could see many rows of neatly marked openings on the side.

"There must be a hundred little rooms in there," he said. "We can use one of them."

"Sam?" Virginia sounded uneasy again. "Are you thinking of hiding inside that particular building?"

"Uh-huh. Is it trapped?"

She went closer to examine the nearest entrance.

"Yes," she said.

He frowned. "Well? Can you untangle it?"

"Yes," she said again very evenly.

He waited for a few seconds, but he did not sense any psi energy. She was staring at the trapped entrance, but she wasn't working.

"What the hell's wrong?" he asked. "It's not like we've got all day here."

She turned slowly to face him. In the green twilight her eyes were more shadowed than the interior of the cubicle.

"Not this one," she said. "Let's try another one."

He started to argue and then reminded himself that when it came to traps, she was the pro. "All right, pick another one, but hurry."

She was already moving down the narrow lane between two looming structures. He paced behind her, controlling his temper when she passed up three more trapped entrances. Silently he willed her to make her choice so that he could get on with the task of rigging up some sort of defense that would protect her while he slept off the afterburn.

She turned at an intersection and went down another lane. Just when he was ready to take charge and make the choice for her, she came to a halt.

"Here," she said. She sounded relieved. "This one is okay. We can go inside."

"About time," he growled. "Do what you have to do."

She glanced at him. "No problem. There's no trap at this entrance."

"Damn." He took a closer look. The doorway she had chosen looked more elaborate than the others. It was wider, more ornately carved. It was taller, too. He shook his head. If push came to shove, it would not be as easy to defend. He turned away, scanning the ranks of darkly glowing openings in the green walls.

"No good," he said brusquely. "Pick one with a trap that you can reset after we're inside. It will give us an extra level of protection."

"This is the only one I've seen that feels okay."

He scowled. "What the hell do you mean, it feels okay?"

"Just what I said. This one is okay." Stubborn determination gleamed in her eyes. "This is my area of expertise, and I'm telling you that this will be a safer place to hide than any of the other possibilities that I've seen so far."

"But it's not even trapped."

"There's something wrong about those traps on the other entrances," she said. "I could untangle them, but I don't think that I should."

"You don't think you *should?*" He wanted to shake her. Didn't she realize he was trying to protect her? "What kind of a reason is that? If we get cornered in this chamber by a couple of hunters trying to protect an illegal excavation site, we're going to need all the help we can get. I want a doorway that's well-trapped."

She wrapped her arms around herself and looked at him with unshakable conviction. "We can't go into any of those other rooms. Trust me on this, Sam. This is the only chamber I've seen yet that feels safe."

He hesitated. "Safe?"

"Yes." She unhugged herself and touched his cheek. She dropped her hand immediately when he flinched. "Sam, we've got to get you inside. You're in bad shape. You're scaring me."

"Just don't touch me," he warned. "Not until I've slept this off."

"Don't be ridiculous. How can it hurt if I touch you? Sam, you're not yourself. If you've got an ounce of sense, you'll admit that you're in no condition to be in charge of the firm of Gage & Burch at the moment."

She was right, but he did not want to admit it. Another wave of shivering swept over him. "Find a trapped room."

"We don't have time to keep looking. You need sleep."

"In a while. Not just yet."

"I'm officially declaring myself the boss of this partnership, at least for now. And I say you need sleep. Come with me."

She reached out without warning. Her hand closed around his arm, sending a tide of sensation screaming through his senses. This time he knew he was lost. The raging hunger roared past the last of his defenses. A great shudder of need wracked him. He no longer possessed the will to resist.

When she tugged him gently toward the doorway, he lurched once and then stumbled after her. At that moment he would have followed her anywhere; straight into hell, if that was where she wished to lead him.

She seemed oblivious to the storm that had him in its grip. She drew him through the untrapped doorway into a wide, softly lit room. He was vaguely aware of a tall piece of statuary in the center of the space. It soared toward the ceiling, delicately carved in the familiar airy, abstract designs the Harmonics had favored. There was a shallow pool beneath it. Emerald streams of sparkling energy poured gently from the top of the ornately designed quartz. The gentle waves bounced and splashed in the pool.

"A fountain," Virginia breathed in wonder. "I've never seen anything like it. Never even *heard* of anything like it. Maybe this place was some sort of park, or maybe it was a garden in some wealthy Harmonic home. But why all the little tiny rooms in that warren outside?"

"Maybe the neighborhood went bad. Turned into a slum." Sam shook his head, unable to concentrate on the fountain or any of the other questions she had brought up. All of his over-rezzed senses were riveted on her.

"This way," she said.

He did not reply. He knew that he was so far gone now, that if he tried to speak, nothing coherent would come from his throat. He stared longingly at the back of her head as she urged him through an interior doorway. She had a beautifully shaped head, he decided. And the color of her hair, a warm reddish brown, was perfect. The urge to pull her down onto the hard quartz floor and cover her body with his own was nearly overwhelming. He prayed that he would crash into deep sleep before he succumbed to the torrent of desire that was pulsing through him.

Inside the smaller antechamber, Virginia paused. "This will do, I think. You can sleep it off here."

He caught a glimpse of some large chests arranged around the room, saw a green staircase in the corner, but all he could think of was Virginia. He closed his eyes to shut out the sight of her. The attempt to banish her vision from his senses did not work. The scent of her hit him like a narcotic.

Crash, he thought. *Just crash, and this will all be over.* Then he remembered something else; something he had to do first. He reached into his boot and removed the slender little mag-rez gun. He held it out to her.

"Take this. If anyone comes through the door of this chamber before I wake up, use it."

She looked at the gun and then raised startled eyes to his. "Since when did you start carrying a mag-rez?"

"Since I ran into my first ruin rat on my very first consulting assignment," he said brusquely. "I nearly got myself killed. After that, I started carrying one. I also carry a flashlight, even though no one's ever found a darkened tunnel, and extra tuned amber. Call me superstitious. Do you know how to use this?"

"No, of course not," she said primly. "Instruction in the use of mag-rez weapons is not included in the curriculum of the department of archaeology at the university. Probably because it's illegal to carry one underground."

He gritted his teeth and pointed at the weapon. "This is the safety. Disengage it before you use it. When you want to fire, just point it in the general direction of that doorway and squeeze the trigger. Don't worry about aiming. This thing will stun a man regardless of where you hit him.''

She looked dubious. "Do you really think I'll need it?"

"I can't think clearly at all right now," he said flatly. "So just take it and promise me you'll use it if necessary."

"Okay." Gingerly she took it from his hand.

He looked around for a place to lie down. But he was still humming with afterburn sizzle and the sexual energy continued to wash through him. It would be a few more minutes before he could take refuge in sleep. He closed his eyes, fighting back raw need. When he raised his lashes, he saw that Virginia was watching him with intense concern.

"Sam?"

"I want you."

She blinked but she did not draw back.

"Sorry," he muttered. He wiped his damp forehead with the back of his sleeve. "Can't help it."

"I know." There was no fear in her eyes, but there was something else; something that could have been sad resignation. "It's all right. I understand about the effects of the afterburn."

"The hell with the afterburn." Unable to keep his hands off her any longer, he gripped her shoulders. "I've wanted you since the day you walked through my front door."

She stared at him with what could only have been amazement. "You have?"

He groaned, pulled her hard against his chest, and tilted her chin. "More than I've ever wanted anything or anyone else in my life."

He kissed her before she could respond. He had to kiss her. Just one kiss, he promised himself. Drain off a little of the sexual charge. By the time it was over, surely the crash would have overtaken him. It had to hit soon. Any second now. Then he would escape into the merciful oblivion of sleep before he did anything else real stupid.

As a plan, it seemed simple and straightforward. Then again, he might have been hallucinating by now, he thought.

But however brilliant the scheme seemed, he knew as soon as he took her mouth that something was going horribly, wonderfully, terrifyingly wrong. Virginia put her arms around his neck and kissed him back.

"Oh, *Sam.*"

"Oh, *shit.*"

Her response was the last straw. He cradled her face in his hands and drank hungrily from her lips as if he could consume the essence of her vibrant spirit. She moaned softly and tightened her grip on his neck. He could feel the swell of her breasts beneath the sturdy twill of her shirt. The inside of her mouth was warm and welcoming, just as he had imagined.

For the first time he feared that the crash would overcome him before he could finish what he had started. A whole new sense of urgency slammed through him.

Not daring to raise his mouth from hers for fear that he might somehow lose her, he started to undress her. It was not an easy task. His hands were shaking so badly that he could barely manage the buttons.

He felt her fingers slide beneath the waistband of his trousers, gliding up beneath the hem of his shirt. Her palms flattened against his chest, and he thought he would go through the roof. He realized that she was shivering now, too.

"Sam, are you sure you're not ill?"

"I'm okay." He struggled with her shirt.

"I was so afraid that you—"

"Nothing to be afraid of." He managed to wrench his mouth from hers long enough to kiss her throat. "I swear it. You don't have to be afraid of me. I won't hurt you. I could never hurt you."

"I know. That wasn't what I meant."

He finished fumbling with the last of the buttons that closed her shirt. He peeled the garment off her shoulders and hurled it aside. Then he heard himself utter a thick, husky groan. He could feel her firm little nipples pressing against the sleek fabric of her bra.

She was working on his belt now. The sweet torture was almost beyond endurance. Every time her fingers brushed against his skin he thought he would explode.

He dragged the straps of her bra down her arms, freeing her breasts. He leaned his hot forehead against her cool brow and looked at the taut, peaked curves.

"You are so beautiful," he muttered, awed.

She gave him a smile laced with infinite mystery. "No, but you're making me feel beautiful."

He lacked the patience to argue. She was beautiful; the most beautiful, most desirable woman he had ever seen in his life. He knew that, even if she did not.

He scooped her up in his arms, intending to lower her to the floor. Out of the corner of his eye, he saw a wide chest carved of quartz. It would not be any softer than the floor, but at least it looked vaguely like a bed.

He carried Virginia to the hard couch and put her down on it. She lay back on the emerald stone, her hair spilling around her head, her eyes glowing with desire, and watched him with great expectation as he unbuckled his belt.

Her expression nearly finished him.

He yanked impatiently at his clothing. The cocktail in his bloodstream made him clumsy and awkward. But when he finally lowered himself onto the chest and pulled Virginia into his arms, he had never felt better in his life.

Nothing had ever been this good.

He slid one leg between hers and dampened his fingers in her liquid heat.

She gasped, trembled, and closed her eyes. She slid her palm down his chest, across his belly, and lower. He felt her fingers close around him and thought his heart might stop.

"*Sam.*"

Another wave of need thundered through him. "No, don't touch me like that. I won't be able—"

"It's all right."

"Stop saying that." He came down on top of her. Her green-gold eyes were luminous with desire. "Virginia, this isn't the way I wanted to do this, but I can't wait. Not this time."

"It's all right," she said. She opened her legs for him, drew up her knees, and wrapped her arms around him. "Really."

"Hold me." It was half plea, half demand. "Promise me you won't let go."

"Never."

He squeezed his eyes shut against the riptide of need that was threatening to sweep him out into a dark sea. She shifted a little beneath him, and the glide of her silken skin against him nearly ended the matter right then and there.

He plunged deep; sinking recklessly, exultantly into the snug, tight channel of her body. He felt the initial resistance and then she closed around him. She cried out and clung to him, fighting him for the embrace.

He rocked violently against her, driving himself to the hilt with every thrust, needing to forge a bond that would hold long after this encounter.

The climax hit him. Simultaneously he thought he felt Virginia convulse beneath him, but he could not be certain. He barely had time to register a sensation so intense that it could not truly be described as pleasure. But it was not pain, either. Something else, he thought vaguely, something infinitely more important.

There was no time to analyze the incredible feeling. Hard on its heels came the crash. He could only marvel that it had not struck sooner.

He collapsed on top of her, aware that he was trapping her against the quartz chest with his weight. But there was nothing he could do about it. The deep, dreamless sleep took him.

Four

It felt as if one of the ancient stone corridors had caved in on top of her. Sam was no lightweight to begin with and, as she quickly discovered, he seemed to be built mostly of muscle and bone. There was no softness in him and there was none beneath her.

Talk about being between a rock and a hard place, Virginia thought.

She took a deep breath, braced her hands on Sam's chest, and heaved upward with all of her strength. She managed to gain some wiggle room and, with another strong shove, she was finally able to slide out from underneath his inert body.

She sat up and got cautiously to her feet. There was something wrong with her knees. They were not quite steady. A tremor went through her. She had to grab hold of the edge of the chest to get her balance. *For the record, Adeline, everything you've ever heard about sex with a ghost-hunter in the midst of an afterburn is true.*

Or maybe this was just the result of sex with Sam, she thought cheerfully. She didn't have an extensive amount of experience to call upon when it came to this kind of thing, but it didn't take a lot of experimentation to know what she'd just shared with Sam had been very special. At least she no longer entertained any doubts as to whether or not there were fires of passion burning somewhere inside Sam.

They were there, all right. Enough to set a whole forest ablaze.

Of course, his response to her could have been ignited simply by the legendary ghost-hunter buzz, she reminded herself. Her euphoric spirits sank as suddenly as they had risen. Anything in skirts might have had the same impact on him at that particular moment.

Reality returned with a jarring thud. With a sigh, she steadied herself and glanced around the gloom-filled room. The carved stone chest on which Sam slept was one of several in the chamber. There were also a variety of vases and urns set in softly glowing alcoves. The drenching shadows created a solemn but surprisingly tranquil effect. Perhaps this had once been a meditation room in a Harmonic home. Assuming the Harmonics had meditated.

Questions, questions.

She dressed quickly and picked up the little mag-rez gun. She checked the safety as Sam had demonstrated and then shoved it into her belt.

She glanced uncertainly at Sam. He certainly looked magnificent stretched out stark naked on the stone chest, and she knew he was not cold because the temperature in the catacombs was always the same, comfortable and dry, day and night, year in, year out. But the sight of him was more than a little distracting. The muscled, well-defined contours of his chest and shoulders sent a pleasant little shiver through her.

Their lovemaking had been fast and furious. There had been no time for her to indulge herself in an exploration of his body. She had been intensely aware of the thick, heavy size and weight of his erection, but she had not really *seen* him. Now, she could not stop gazing at him. He fascinated her, she thought. She had wanted to stroke him and touch him for weeks, but this was the first opportunity she'd had to satisfy her longing.

She examined the fierce planes of his face, relishing the determined angle of his jaw and the pleasing, masculine shape of his ears. His dark hair was seductively ruffled where she had run her fingers through it earlier. With his eyes closed he was all hard edges and tough, sleek male. But when his eyes were open you saw the intelligence and the self-control that defined his nature.

When Sam loved, she thought, his emotions would be as steady and as enduring as the glow of Harmonic quartz.

Unable to resist the temptation, she reached out very carefully and slowly closed her hand around the top of his muscled thigh. He was hard and warm beneath her fingers. She drew her palm slowly down to his knee, savoring the feel of him.

Sam shuddered and mumbled something in his sleep. Startled, she snatched her hand away and stepped back. But when he did not awaken, she reached out once more.

This time she traced a path upward toward his chest, curling her fingers in the crisp hair there. He shifted slightly, but she knew from the steadiness of his breathing that he was still sound asleep. A part of him was stirring, she noticed. She stared at his penis, fascinated to see that it appeared to be swelling in length and width once more. Apparently, the deep sleep of afterburn did not shut down all systems.

There was probably a law against looking at him like this, she thought. If there wasn't, there should have been. It was entirely too much fun.

On the other hand, she was going to marry him soon. Surely that gave her some rights.

"Enough with the voyeuristic fun and games," she muttered. "You're supposed to be standing guard."

She picked up Sam's discarded clothing and covered his torso with his shirt. Then she folded his trousers and placed them neatly beneath his head to serve as a pillow. She was already starting to feel quite wifely, she thought, amused.

With a last glance at him, she turned and walked out into the fountain room. The green energy continued to flow and splash in the small pool. It had no doubt been doing so for several thousand years.

She braced one hand on the thick edge of the doorway and looked around with professional interest. This room had the same somber, curiously reflective feel as the smaller antechamber in which Sam slept. She could not explain, even to herself, why these spaces felt safe while the countless little cubicles outside did not.

She took her hand off the wall and made her way across the fountain room to the outer door. She gazed into the narrow aisle that separated this block of cells from the one across the way and listened intently with both her physical and para senses.

Nothing. No indication that the unusual trap that guarded the main entrance to this weird complex had been breached. No voices or footsteps echoed on the paths that intersected the ranks of cubicle-laced buildings. She detected nothing that indicated that anyone who might be looking for them had discovered the zoo chamber.

She waited quietly in the fountain room for a while longer, uncomfortably aware of the weight of the mag-rez gun on her hip. Gradually, boredom set in. Professional curiosity followed closely on its heels. Whatever this place was, it constituted a spectacular new find. She had a degree in para-archaeology, and she was diligent about keeping up with the research on the subject. She was quite certain that nothing remotely resembling this nest of tiny, illusion-trapped cubicles had ever been written up in the academic literature.

She stepped cautiously out into the shadowy lane, visions of an article in the *Journal of Para-Archaeology* with her name on it as author dancing in her head. That kind of publicity would do wonders for the reputation of the new firm of Gage & Burch.

She walked slowly along the gloom-filled path and paused in front of the first of the small cells that lined the little alley. She examined the dense shadow that glinted just at the edge of her vision. The human eye could detect the stuff that the Harmonics had used to weave their dangerous snares, but it could not focus directly on the nearly invisible psi energy.

She crouched down, concentrating with her para senses, and probed the pattern. As she had concluded earlier, there was nothing particularly complex about the design. She could undo it easily enough. But the sense of wrongness was deeply disturbing. Everything within her resisted the notion of untangling the trap.

With a shock, it occurred to her that perhaps it was not the trap itself that was dangerous. Maybe the true threat existed— or had once existed—*inside* the little room. Perhaps the trap was just a warning.

Maybe this place had once been a Harmonic hotel and all of these little traps were nothing more than ordinary Do Not Disturb signs hung on doorknobs to keep the maid from entering unexpectedly.

She contemplated that possibility for a moment and then returned to her zoo theory. She liked it much better. The traps might have functioned as fences to keep dangerous creatures locked inside or to keep curious visitors from getting too close to the beasts inside the cages.

She straightened and walked a few more feet to examine some of the other illusion-darkened entrances. Every single one of them gave off the same clear psychic warnings.

After a while, she returned to the fountain room. A quick check on Sam showed that he was still totally out of it.

She sat down on a glowing quartz bench facing the untrapped doorway and took the mag-rez gun out of her belt.

She wondered how long Sam would sleep.

• • •

Sam came awake with a sense of urgency, as if someone had just yelled *fire*. He sat up quickly, memory returning in a heated rush. But there was nothing to indicate that the situation had changed while he had slept off the worst effects of the afterburn. If any of Leon Drummond's pals had burst through the doorway, he would have awakened with his hands and feet bound in duct tape, if he had awakened at all.

Relief swept through him. Something soft slid off his chest and fell to the floor. He looked down and saw his shirt. Virginia must have covered him with it after he had nodded off, which had been right after he had taken her with all the finesse of a specter-cat in full rut.

Virginia. He briefly closed his eyes as the images cascaded through him, burning more intensely than ghost fire. For a few seconds he savored them. Then reality closed in. He knew that his recollection of her passionate response might be nothing more than an illusion concocted by his singed senses; some sort of weird para-psych rationalization for what he had done to her.

Yet he could still feel the softness of the skin on the insides of her thighs and the damp, clinging clasp of her body. Just remembering made his insides tighten all over again.

He had wanted her more than he had ever thought it possible to want any woman. But no more so because of the buzz from the afterburn. The truth was, he had been wanting her just as badly for weeks. The only difference was that two hours ago he had lost control.

The flash of relief he had experienced after waking evaporated. In its place was a bottomless pool of dread. He had to face the grim truth: After weeks of being so cautious, so careful, there was a damn good chance that he had destroyed the glowing future he had worked so hard to build.

He had no one to blame but himself.

Virginia had had a bad case of bridal jitters before they

embarked on this venture. After what he had done to her here in this room, she no doubt despised him. It would be a miracle if he hadn't scared the living daylights out of her. She was probably making plans this very minute not only to call off their marriage but their business partnership as well.

He picked up his shirt and got to his feet. Anger washed through him. He was furious with himself. The loss of control had been inexcusable. He could only pray that he had not hurt her.

How long had he been out? He glanced at his watch. Two hours. Long enough to restore some but not all of his depleted psi energy. He needed more sleep to function at full capacity but he could manage with what he had regained during the nap.

He grabbed his trousers and pulled them on. The only thing he could do to make amends to Virginia was to get her safely back to the surface.

A shadow moved in the doorway that separated the antechamber from the fountain room. Not illusion-shadow, but it might as well have been, given the hopelessness of his situation.

"Sam." Virginia hovered anxiously in the doorway. "You're awake. Everything okay?"

"Good enough." He realized with a jolt that he did not want to meet her eyes. He did not want to see the accusation and the wariness that he knew he would find there. "Nothing new outside?"

"We're still alone in this place. I'm beginning to think I was right when I suggested it might have once been a zoo. Something about the nature of the traps makes me think they were set to keep visitors away from whatever used to live in all these little apartments or cages."

"Whoever or whatever once lived in the cells is long gone." He reached for his boots. He did not remember removing them. His jaw tightened. "Got the mag-rez?"

"Right here." She took a few steps into the room to hand it to him. "Sam, are you really okay?"

"Don't worry, I'll be able to get us out of here." He took the narrow little gun from her and shoved it back into his belt. "There's probably another exit around here somewhere, but I think our best bet is to go back out the way we came."

She halted. "Back through the waterfall?"

"Yeah. It's the last thing Drummond would expect. Especially after all this time has passed. By now he'll have reported us officially missing, probably killed by an explosion of dissonance energy. I doubt if we'll find him hanging around on the other side waiting for us. But just in case, I'll have the mag-rez in my hand when we go through the waterfall."

"All right. Whatever you think best. You're the expert on ghost-energy."

He glanced down and realized that he was dressed. He could find no more excuses for avoiding her eyes. Time to act like a man. He turned slowly around to face her. "Virginia—"

"Sam—"

They both broke off, staring at each other. In the gloom it was impossible for him to read the expression in her eyes. If she was frightened of him, she was hiding it well, he thought.

He braced himself and tried again. "I'm sorry for what happened," he said evenly. "I don't know what else to say. I could promise you that it won't ever happen again, but I don't know if I can keep that promise."

She did not pretend to misunderstand. "I see."

He drew a deep breath. "I realize that you're probably having second thoughts about our business arrangement as well as our marriage. I don't blame you. I've been doing some thinking about it, too."

"You have?"

He glanced around the tranquil little room. "This is not the time or place to talk about how we're going to terminate our business futures."

"No, it's not." There was an unsettling, flat note in her voice.

"Yeah, well, let's save that conversation for later." He started toward the door, aware that even in the depths of the disaster, he was still trying to buy himself some time. The odds were strongly against him coming up with a way to talk her into going through with the marriage after what had happened, but he could not give up without a fight.

She looked at him as he went past her. "Sam, do you really regret what happened?"

"Hell, yes, I regret it." He planted one hand against the green stone doorway and turned to face her. "Making love to you was the last thing I wanted to do."

She stiffened. "I realize that you were rezzed up because of the afterburn."

"That was no excuse."

"Just tell me one thing. Would anything in skirts have worked for you two hours ago?"

He frowned at her trousers. "You aren't wearing skirts."

She narrowed her eyes. "That was a figure of speech."

"It's never smart to use figures of speech when you're talking to a hunter who's still recovering from an afterburn. We tend to be literal, even on our good days."

"For heaven's sake, this is no time for wisecracks. We're talking about our future."

"I thought we just got through deciding to talk about it later." He took his hand off the wall and stalked into the fountain room.

"Damn it," she called out behind him, "don't you dare walk out on me when I'm talking to you. Come back here, Sam Gage."

"What the hell do you want from me?" He felt his temper ignite. "I said I'm sorry. I don't usually lose control, not even during an afterburn. But things got out of hand this time."

She swept out her palm to indicate the quartz chest on

which they had made love. "Didn't what happened in here mean *anything* to you?"

"Of course it did. It meant I screwed up everything. But what's done is done."

She raised her chin, eyes glittering with anger. "Would you undo it if you could?"

"Didn't I just get through saying that I—" He broke off abruptly. There was no point lying about it. The damage was done. He set his back teeth. "I wish it had happened under other circumstances. I wish I had done things differently. I wish I hadn't scared the hell out of you."

"But you aren't really, truly sorry that you made love to me?"

He hesitated. "Well—"

"Just say it."

He felt cornered. Despair, anger, and frustration boiled together, a dangerous stew spiced with emotions he knew he did not handle well. "You want the truth? The truth is what I said to you just before I tossed you down onto that damned stone chest. The truth is that I've been wanting to make love to you since the first day I saw you."

A short, intense silence gripped the chamber.

Virginia's brows bristled in a ferocious scowl. "Good. Because that's pretty much how I've felt from the first moment I saw you, too."

He felt as if he'd just been struck by lightning. For a few seconds he was too stunned to do anything more than stare at her. "It is?

"Yes." She glared at him. "But you seemed so distant and cool. So businesslike. You kept talking about how many new clients we would attract working as a team. You went on and on about how much money we'd both make once we sold the house to developers."

He finally managed to unfreeze himself. He took a step toward her. "I never wanted to sell the house in the first place.

I came up with the idea because I thought it would be a good way to talk you into a marriage-of-convenience. I figured if I—'' He stopped. ''Hell, I don't know what I was thinking.''

She cleared her throat. ''We're both adults. We're single. There's no reason we can't simply admit that we're attracted to each other. Marriages-of-convenience are designed for just this sort of situation.''

''A legal, socially acceptable, two-year affair.''

''Exactly.'' She shrugged. ''If it's just passion, it will probably burn itself out in that length of time.''

''Yeah. Sure.'' Never in a million years. How could he possibly let go of her in two years? Better not to go there in the first place if he knew that he would eventually lose her. But how could he not take what she offered, given the lonely alternative. ''Virginia—''

''That's what you wanted, wasn't it? That was the deal. A two-year MC.'' She smiled a little too brightly. ''And I agreed.''

She was acting weird, and it made him more uneasy than ever. What the hell was the matter with him? He had gotten exactly what he'd asked for, what he'd wished for when he'd concocted the plan in the first place.

''You know, you were right when you said that this was not the time or place to discuss this sort of thing,'' Virginia said briskly. ''We'd better get going.''

He moved toward her. ''Is sex all you want out of this?''

''Isn't that what you want out of it?''

''Sex is good. Great.'' Anger pulsed in him. ''I can work with sex.''

Her face tightened in renewed concern. ''You know, you really don't look normal yet, Sam. You could still be suffering from afterburn. Maybe you'd better get some more sleep before we attempt to go back through that waterfall.''

''You're right about one thing. I'm not feeling real normal.''

Her eyes widened as he closed the distance between them. "Now hold on just one damn minute. If you think we're going to have sex every time you claim to be in the throes of an afterburn buzz, you can think again. I'll admit it's interesting, but—"

She stopped talking abruptly when he caught her wrists and pinned her to the wall.

"You just got through telling me that you were in this deal for the sex," he reminded her.

"I've got nothing against sex." Her voice was tight with anger. "But the next time we do it, I want to make sure it's for real. Not just the result of a bad burn buzz. Don't you get it?"

"No." He leaned in closer. "Explain it to me in short words."

"I want to be sure it's me you want. I want to be absolutely certain that not just any female would do."

"Trust me, no one else will do."

There was a short, tense silence. Then she cleared her throat and wriggled her fingers in his grasp. "In that case, stop acting like some macho jerk hunter."

He kept her wrists anchored against the wall. "But I am a macho jerk hunter."

"No, you are not," she muttered, seriously disgruntled now. "Stop talking like that."

"You've as good as said I behaved like a macho jerk hunter a couple of hours ago when I made love to you just before I crashed. What happens the next time we get into this kind of situation? Am I going to have to listen to a lot of accusations about how anything in skirts would do? When it's over, will I have to explain that I knew it was you I was having sex with?"

"Just because I wanted to be sure you knew it was me—"

"Believe me. I knew it was you. Just like I know it's you now."

He kissed her, hard and deliberately, letting her feel the frustration and temper she had aroused in him, letting her know that this time he knew full well that she was the woman he had pinned against the glowing quartz wall.

She went rigid. Despair knifed through him.

"Virginia." He released her wrists and caught her head between his hands. "Damn it, Virginia. I want you so much."

She gave a muffled cry and threw her arms around his neck, kissing him feverishly. "I didn't mean to call you a stupid, macho jerk hunter."

"Don't worry about it." Relief surged through him. "Sometimes I am a macho jerk hunter."

"No." She clenched her fingers in his hair. "Never. I knew from the first day that you weren't a macho jerk hunter."

"Yeah?" He took her tender earlobe between his teeth and nibbled hungrily. "What was your first clue?"

"You were reading the *Journal of Para-Archaeology* instead of the latest issue of *Sex-Starved Psychic Playmates*."

"Lucky for me my subscription ran out three months ago," he said very fervently against her throat. "I never got around to renewing it."

She laughed softly. Her head tipped back against his arm. "Oh, Sam, do you really think this will work?"

"We'll make it work." Two years. He had two full years to make it work. He touched the edge of his tongue to the soft skin beneath the collar of her shirt.

She stiffened.

"Sam?"

"It's okay. Even without the skirts, I'm positive I'm dealing with the right lady here."

"No, wait." She planted her palms against his shoulders and pushed him away from her.

He stilled, aware that something was wrong. "What is it?"

"Psi energy. I can feel it. Someone is trying to take down the big trap at the entrance to this zoo."

"Drummond's friends. So they did come looking, after all." The charge of sexual anticipation that had been arcing through him instantly transmuted itself into another kind of high-rez buzz.

"Wait here." He turned and went swiftly across the fountain room. He halted in the outer doorway and listened intently. Sound carried underground. So did the feel of psi energy.

He heard voices reverberating in the distance. They came from the vicinity of the entrance to the vast zoo chamber.

". . . waste of time. Don't care what Drummond says. No way the S.O.B. coulda made it through that waterfall with the little lady tangler. No small-time security guy could be that good. Even if he was that good and even if he did make it through with her, he'd have one hell of an afterburn. He'll be wasted for at least another hour or two."

"We're working for Fairbanks, not Drummond. He said not to take any chances, and he's the one paying us. The orders were to check out every possibility in this damned corridor, so that's what we're gonna do. Now, shut up and untangle this trap."

"Okay, okay. Give me a minute. It's a big sucker."

Sam left the doorway and went to where Virginia stood waiting.

"Let's go." He took her arm.

"Where?"

"Up." He took her arm and started toward the emerald staircase. "It's easier to hunt when you've got the high ground."

"Whatever you say."

She followed him up the narrow, twisting steps to the next level. He saw the gloom-shrouded entrance to another chamber similar to the one below. An energy fountain cascaded silently in the center. Several more ornately carved chests were arranged in an artful manner around the room.

But the thing that interested him the most was the narrow window. He hesitated before he crossed the threshold and glanced at Virginia.

"Trapped?"

She shook her head, frowning intently. "No. This room is clear. Maybe this was the zoo's souvenir shop."

"Or the visitors' room in the prison." He went to the window, braced one hand on the wide ledge, and looked down into the lane. "This will work. If they bother to search this far, I'll have a clear shot."

". . . Got it. We're in."

"Shit. What the hell is this place? Look at all those little rooms. Some kinda cheap hotel, d'ya think?"

Virginia stirred hesitantly in the doorway. Then she walked slowly into the room, careful to keep a respectful distance from the energy fountain. "I don't like this."

"Don't worry. I've got a hunch that once they get a good look at all these little cubicles and realize how long it will take to search this place, they'll figure out something else to do. If they do get this far, I can handle them."

"I know that." She folded her arms very tightly beneath her breasts. "Sam, I'm afraid that tangler will try to de-rez some of the traps."

He sank deeper into the gloom and watched the lane. "So?"

"I told you, I don't think they should be touched. If he starts fooling around with some of them, looking for us—"

She broke off.

He gazed at her. "You're really worried about the nature of the those illusion traps, aren't you?"

"Yes." Her mouth tightened. "I told you, there's something very, very strange about them. One way or another, they all seem to spell out Do Not Disturb in great big capital letters.

"Whatever didn't want to be disturbed is long gone, Virginia."

"I know, but it just doesn't *feel* right."

He shrugged. "Maybe that tangler down there will come to the same conclusion, and he and his hunter pal will leave us in peace."

". . . Gonna take a couple of hours to go through this place room by room. Must be hundreds of little cubicles in here. And they're all trapped, I'm telling you."

"If they got this far, neither one of 'em would be in great shape. Gage will have crashed, and the tangler will be scared out of her wits. I'll bet they would have picked one of these little cubbyholes near the entrance. Start working, man. I'd rather find the bastard before he recovers from the crash. Easier to handle that way."

"Uh, Drake, I don't like the looks of these traps."

"I don't give a damn how they look to you. Start takin' 'em apart."

"There's something real weird—"

"Shut up and get to work, Chaz. Unless you wanna explain things to Fairbanks."

"Sure. Okay. I'm workin' on it."

"Oh, damn," Virginia whispered. "He's going to do it."

Sam took his eyes off the lane long enough to look at her. The stark alarm in her voice worried him. She was scared, he thought. Genuinely, thoroughly, deep-down scared.

"What is it with you and these traps?" he started to ask.

"*Sam.*" Her eyes widened in sudden alarm. "Get down. Now."

"Take it easy, honey, I've got to keep watch—"

"He's got it. He's undone the first trap. I can feel it."

"It's okay—"

"No, it's not okay." She flew toward him across the room and seized his arm. "Get away from the window."

Automatically, he started to resist the tug of her fingers. But the urgency in her was not to be ignored. He reminded himself that traps fell into her area of expertise. They were partners. He had to respect her instincts.

He allowed himself to be drawn away from the window. She pulled him deeper into the room.

"Down," she whispered, dragging him down behind a large quartz chest. "Hurry."

He crouched beside her, the mag-rez gun in hand. "I hope you know what the hell you're doing."

Before she could respond, an inhuman shriek of mingled rage and despair rent the gloom of the alien zoo. It echoed endlessly off the walls. Sam froze, his hand tightening convulsively around the gun. Beside him, Virginia shuddered.

"What in the name of Old Earth . . . ?" Sam whispered.

A very human shout went up, a high, keening cry of terror.

"There's something in there."

Chaz, the tangler, Sam thought.

". . . Get outa here . . ."

Another alien scream rose, joining the crescendoing wail of the first. And then a torrent of screeches, shrieks, howls, and dreadful cries arose. There was a hellishly mournful quality to the unnatural sounds, as though whatever had once inhabited the small cells had been aroused from their centuries-deep sleep to protest the disturbance. The cacophony of otherworldly cries drowned out the screams of Chaz and Drake.

The vast zoo room began to darken. The green gloom seemed to thicken and grow dense. Sam followed Virginia's gaze. They both looked out the narrow window. It was like looking into the depths of an alien sea.

"Dear heaven." Virginia said in amazement.

He knew what was going through her mind. There was no such thing as night and day in the ruins. The glow of the quartz was always steady. True, there had been more than the usual number of shadows in the zoo chamber, but there had been light, and it had remained at a constant level.

Until now.

Only the chamber in which they crouched remained luminous.

Jagged shards of green lightning flashed outside the narrow opening, shattering the heavy darkness that enveloped the zoo. The alien shrieks grew louder.

More lightning sizzled. As Sam watched, an acid-hued bolt of energy illuminated some thing that floated in midair outside the window. He caught a glimpse of a green phantom so gossamer thin and transparent that he could see straight through it to the opposite wall. As he watched, another specter joined the first.

"UDEMs," Virginia whispered. "When Chaz untangled the trap he must have disturbed some."

"Whatever the hell those two things are, they aren't standard-issue energy ghosts." Sam probed cautiously, feeling for the telltale trace of psi energy emitted by normal unstable dissonance energy manifestations. What he picked up with his para senses felt wrong. He cut off the probe immediately. He did not want to draw the attention of the strange specters.

"If they're not UDEMs, what are they?" she asked very softly.

"They're energy ghosts of some kind but not like any I've ever dealt with. Look at the way they move."

"As if—" Virginia hesitated. "As if they're headed somewhere."

"Yeah. Right toward Chaz and Drake."

"But that's impossible."

"Uh-huh."

She was right, of course. UDEMs were not sentient beings. They certainly weren't the ghosts of long-dead aliens, although more than one or two hucksters and con men had tried to convince the gullible of that over the years.

Technically speaking, UDEMS were nothing more than

balls of residual psi energy left behind by whatever had once powered Harmonic technology. The only reason they were called ghosts was because they tended to drift through the ancient corridors like ghosts.

Green lightning zigzagged through the misty darkness outside the window. More ghosts drifted past the opening, streaming toward the entrance of the zoo chamber.

"Damn," Sam said. "What the devil is going on out there?"

"I don't know, but I can tell you that this is Chaz's fault," Virginia said grimly. "He set them off. I knew there was something strange about those traps."

The hideous wails continued to rise and fall in the unnatural night.

"Sounds like a reunion of lost souls," Virginia whispered. "I can't even hear Chaz and Drake now. Wonder what's happened to them?"

"Maybe we don't want to know."

"Maybe you're right."

Virginia huddled close, but Sam noticed that she was careful not to impede his gun hand. Not that the mag-rez would be effective against whatever was out there, he thought. If one of the things changed course and drifted through the window, their only hope would be his psi-talent.

More lightning sparked violently. Again and again it shattered the night. But there was no accompanying roll of thunder, Sam noticed. For some reason that only made the energy flashes seem all the more bizarre.

"It's like there's a storm going on out there," Virginia muttered.

"Maybe that's exactly what it is," Sam said, thinking about it. "An energy storm triggered by the untangling of the first trap."

"But to what purpose?"

"Who knows? We're talking about the Harmonics here. No one has a clue about why they did anything. If the place was a zoo or a prison, it's possible those in charge installed some unusual security measures. Maybe we're witnessing some kind of system meant to round up the escapees."

"*Sam.*" Virginia touched his arm, her eyes fixed on the window. "Look."

"I see it."

One of the phantoms had halted in front of the opening. Sam told himself that it was just a mindless UDEM, but it was all too easy to imagine that it was peering into this room as if it sensed prey.

He readied himself, not wanting to use psi energy unless there was no alternative, because he could not be sure that his talent would work against this stuff.

The ghost hovered. The brightest portion of it was at least three feet in length, but its aura flared out in a much wider band of acid green.

It drifted through the window.

"Damn."

Beside him, Virginia sucked in a deep breath, but she said nothing.

Decision time, Sam thought. He could either try to prod it back out the window or he could attempt to clobber it. He opted for the gentle nudge.

He sent out a pulse of psi-talent, gently summoning energy from the quartz walls, ceiling, and floor. A small ball of glowing green fire took shape in the center of the room. He propelled it gently toward the intruder.

The strange UDEM that had drifted through the window paused as though confused. Then, to Sam's enormous relief, it retreated from the smaller ghost.

It wafted back out through the window and disappeared in the wake of the school of phantoms roaming through the streets of the zoo.

Virginia exhaled on a long, soft sigh. "Nice. Very nice."

He could almost taste his own relief. For the first time, he realized that his shirt was stuck to his back. "Don't ever say I don't know how to show a lady a fun time on Halloween."

"A lot of hunters would have tried to blast it to smithereens," she said very seriously. "For some reason, I don't think that tactic would have worked."

"No," he said, "I don't think it would have."

The storm crackled and blazed. An endless parade of desolate-sounding specters and phantoms flitted past the window.

The tempest seemed to rage for hours, but when at last it began to abate, Sam looked at his watch. He was startled to see that only twenty-three minutes had passed.

"I think it's ending," Virginia said.

Gradually, the unholy wails receded. The flashes of lightning grew pale, then ceased altogether. As if some invisible hand had flipped a switch, the familiar green glow seeped back into the atmosphere. The strange darkness retreated into the pooling shadows from which it had come.

"Must have seemed like an eternity to Chaz and Drake," Virginia whispered.

"It may have turned out to be just that."

"Are you saying you don't think they survived it?"

"I don't know what was going on out there, but whatever it was, they were caught out in the open." Sam smiled slightly. "Thanks to you, we were safe in this room."

He got cautiously to his feet and went to the window. When he looked out he saw that everything looked very much as it had just before the tempest had been triggered.

Virginia stood slowly behind the chest. "Now what?"

"Now we get the heck out of here before someone else sets off another storm." He moved swiftly back toward her. "Ready?"

"If you're waiting for me, you're backing up."

They found Chaz and Drake lying on the floor near the main gate into the zoo. It was obvious that the two desperate men had tried to flee back through it, but something had caused the illusion trap there to reset itself. The energy storm had caught up with the pair before Chaz could untangle the trap a second time.

Virginia hesitated and then went down beside one of the men and checked for a pulse. She looked up in surprise. "He's unconscious, but alive."

"Same here." Sam rifled through the pockets of the man dressed in leather and khaki until he found a guild license and an amber-powered grid locator. "This is all we need. The locator shows three exits in this sector. We won't have to go back through the waterfall, after all."

"What are you going to do with that man's guild license?"

"I'll give it to Mercer Wyatt. He can take it from there." Sam got to his feet. "The guild polices its own."

Virginia gave him an odd look. "You're, uh, friends with the head of Hunter's Guild?"

"Let's just say that Wyatt and I have a nodding acquaintance. He owes me a couple of favors." Sam studied the illusion trap that guarded the exit. "Go ahead and de-rez it. I'll drag these two out of here. We'll leave them in the corridor. Wyatt can send one of his staff to clean up this mess."

Five

"We were worried sick." Adeline helped herself to a leftover black-and-orange cupcake from the plate on Virginia's desk. "First we hear that you and Sam have gone missing in the corridors; a report which, I hasten to add, none of your buddies believed for one tiny minute, because we all know how good you and Sam are; and then we learn that the two of you got zapped by some sort of massive ghost called a waterfall."

"The waterfall part was for real." Virginia rocked back in her chair and took a sip of hot, spiced cider. "But, as you can see, neither of us got zapped."

She peered at her watch, wondering what was keeping Sam. After talking to the police, he had gone to meet with Mercer Wyatt. She had not liked that. It was no secret in Cadence City that Wyatt ran the guild as though it was his own, private fiefdom. A lot of folks, including an editorial writer on the *Cadence Star* considered him no more than one or two steps removed from being a gangster. But she could not argue with the fact that if you were a ghost-hunter, you had to form some sort of business relationship with the guild. She had not asked

Sam just what kind of terms he had worked out with Wyatt. She was not sure she wanted to know.

"So what, exactly, was going on down there in the tunnels?" Adeline asked around a mouthful of cupcake.

"A band of ruin rats headed by a recently fired employee of the University Museum named Fairbanks uncovered a hole-in-the-wall just beneath the museum's basement. They were using it to siphon off some of the museum's holdings. Stuff that had been in storage for years, which might not have been missed for years. If Mac Ewert hadn't accidentally stumbled onto that waterfall and asked us to help him de-rez it, the rats probably would never have been caught."

Holes-in-the-wall were not uncommon. They usually took the form of tiny cracks and fissures through which little more than ambient psi energy could squeeze. But some of the openings in the thick quartz walls and underground corridors were large enough for a man to crawl through. A few were even bigger: eons-old stairwells and empty shafts that no longer ascended anywhere. It was one of those that Fairbanks, a powerful tangler, had discovered while laboring in the basement of the huge museum.

Adeline gazed at her with the look of a professional inquisitor. "What now?"

Virginia shrugged. "The cops take it from here. Last I heard, they'd picked up everyone involved except Leon Drummond. But I doubt if he'll escape. Not with the guild looking for him as well as the police."

"I wasn't talking about your big case. I know the firm of Gage & Burch has closed it. Probably be all over the evening news." Adeline selected a black-and-orange petit four. "I meant what happens now with you and Sam?"

Virginia took another sip of hot cider and contemplated the heavy mist that drifted in the street outside the office window.

She thought about the passion that had exploded between them in the little fountain chamber.

"Good question," she said quietly.

The narrow streets and twisted lanes of the Old Quarter were thick with fog, but that did not deter the throngs of hobgoblins, ghosts, witches, and assorted monsters who had come to the district to celebrate Halloween.

Virginia walked out of the little corner restaurant with Sam at her side shortly after ten. She could feel the stray pulses of psi energy that leaked from the ruins. They seemed stronger than usual tonight. Maybe it was true that the Dead City was more alive at Halloween than at other times. She was aware of constant little frissons across her para senses. Some just tickled; some were more disturbing. But she could not be sure that all of them were caused by ambient Harmonic energy. She knew that some of the ripples were attributable to Sam, who seemed blithely oblivious to the new level of awareness that pulsed between them.

When he had suggested dinner together earlier, she had been sure that he wanted to talk about their future. But the only thing that had been discussed over a bottle of wine and a leisurely meal of tapenade-tossed cheese ravioli and good bread had been their case.

She did not want to hear another word about their case. She was heartily sick and tired of discussing their case.

Sam paused on the restaurant step and eyed the tide of costumed celebrants that flooded the street.

"I don't know about you, but I've had enough of ghosts and goblins for a while," he said. "What do you say we take a shortcut home and drink a private toast to the successful finale of Gage & Burch's first case?"

Home. To talk some more about their stupid case. Virginia steeled herself. "Sam, we need to talk about us."

"I know," he said.

She was so surprised by his casual agreement that she was momentarily speechless. His mouth curved slightly as he took her arm and steered her along a side street, away from the crowds of revelers.

She shoved her gloved hands into the pockets of her coat and slanted him a sidelong glance. His expression was as enigmatic as ever, but she sensed something going on beneath the surface.

She had come to know him better than she had realized during these past few weeks. And much of what she now knew for certain verified her initial impression. Her instincts had been right that first day. The cool, self-contained veneer was a cover for the deep passions, the unyielding determination, and the rock-solid strength that was at the core of this man. If Sam Gage gave you his word of honor, you could take it to the bank.

If Sam Gage ever said he loved you, you could depend on that love forever.

Commitments like that were dangerous things. Sam probably knew that better than anyone else, she thought. Maybe that was why he was so cautious about making them in the first place.

She decided to take the plunge.

"Sam, about our marriage—"

"I don't want an MC," he said bluntly.

That brought her to an abrupt halt in the middle of the sidewalk. She stopped and swung around to face him. "You've changed your mind?"

"Yes." He watched her with unreadable eyes. "It won't work. I can't handle it."

Despair jolted through her. "You can't handle it? But you're the one who suggested it in the first place."

"It was a mistake. I think I knew it all along, but after what happened in the ruins, I'm sure of it."

"I see." She did not know what to say. This was not how

she had anticipated the conversation would end. "I thought that after what had happened, you might feel differently, but I didn't realize—"

"A marriage-of-convenience will drive me crazy," he interrupted. "I don't want—"

He broke off suddenly as a goblin-masked figure in a long black coat stepped out of the shadows. Light gleamed wickedly on a mag-rez gun.

"I'd say trick or treat," Leon Drummond growled behind the hideous mask. "But you haven't got a choice. You're going to get the trick, whether you want it or not."

Virginia caught her breath. Drummond ignored her. She could see the baleful glitter of his eyes through the holes in the mask. His attention was focused on Sam.

"I'm surprised you're still hanging around, Drummond," Sam said. "Wyatt's got men out looking for you."

"You sonofabitch, you screwed up everything," Leon hissed. "We were nearly finished. Two more days and we would have shut down the operation with no one the wiser. The museum wouldn't have missed the pieces we took until the next full audit. But Ewert had to call you in, and you ruined the whole damned project."

"What can I say?" Sam smiled coldly. "It's what I do."

"Well, it's gonna be the last damned thing you do." Drummond raised the mag-rez gun. "Nobody messes with Leon Drummond and gets away with it. Especially not some two-bit private detective."

Leon was concentrating so fiercely that he never even noticed the ball of green energy that was forming rapidly behind him. Virginia was impressed. Not every hunter could summon a ghost outside the Dead City, let alone control it.

The energy ghost flared and pulsed, gathering strength as Leon continued with his tirade.

"Wyatt's security people are watching my house, thanks to you. I can't even get to my car. They're covering the airport, too. I'll have to use the tunnels to get out of Cadence."

"Risky," Sam said, sounding mildly interested. "Not many people get far in the tunnels once they get beyond the mapped sectors. Unpleasant way to go, all alone in a maze filled with traps and ghosts and who knows what else. They say that even if someone survives the experience, he isn't real sane afterward."

"I'll make it." Leon's hand tightened on the mag-rez. "But I'm gonna make sure you pay for what you did first."

The ball of ghost fire was quite large now. The energy aura pulsed outward abruptly, enveloping Leon Drummond. He jerked wildly when the fringes of the green field touched him. His hair stood on end. His mouth parted on a silent scream. The mag-rez fell from his hand and clattered on the pavement.

A few seconds later, Drummond collapsed, unconscious, beside his weapon.

Virginia exhaled slowly. "You really are good, partner."

Sam gave Drummond a dismissive nod and turned back to her.

"Where were we?" he asked.

She swallowed and managed to drag her eyes away from the still and silent Drummond. "I, uh, think we were discussing the fact that you no longer want to get married."

He frowned. "I didn't say that. I said I didn't want a marriage-of-convenience."

"Oh." Her heart was suddenly weightless. "You did say that you were kind of literal on your good days."

"I thought an MC would give you time to get used to the idea of a real marriage," he said with an air of dogged determination. "But I don't think I could take it, knowing that you were just trying me on for size."

"Size? But there's nothing wrong with your size. I already know that you fit. Perfectly."

"I want a commitment. I want kids. I want to know you'll

be there ten, twenty, forty years from now. I don't want to play house with you. I want a home.''

"Oh, Sam, that's what I want, too." She threw herself against him so hard that it was a wonder he did not go down. "Why didn't you say something sooner?"

He caught her close and wrapped his arms around her. "I was afraid I'd scare you off," he said into her hair. "I came up with the deal on the house and the MC plan as a way to make sure I could hold on to you until I could convince you to fall in love with me."

"I fell in love with you the day I rented the office and the apartment."

"Why the hell didn't you say so? Look at all the time we've wasted."

She raised her head and smiled. "How was I to know that you had fallen in love with me? You never said anything. You were always so cool, so controlled. I was beginning to wonder if you ever got excited about anything."

His eyes gleamed. "You want excitement? Let's go home. I guarantee I'll come up with something exciting."

She hesitated, pointing down at Drummond. "What about him?"

Sam groaned. "I guess I'd better make sure Mercer Wyatt sends someone out to collect him. If I leave him here, he's liable to wake up later and make a nuisance of himself."

"Call Wyatt," Virginia smiled, aware of the happiness blossoming deep inside. "I can wait."

Six

The reception following the lengthy, formal covenant wedding service was held in the downstairs offices of Gage & Burch. Virginia's beaming father and brothers toasted the bride and groom so many times that her mother had to call a cab to take them home. Adeline performed brilliantly as a bridal attendant. Mercer Wyatt created a small stir when he showed up with a gift for the newlyweds—a fine, museum-quality Harmonic vase that had to be worth several thousand dollars. Virginia made a mental note to ask Sam the precise nature of the favors he had done for the head of the guild.

When it was all over, Sam insisted on carrying Virginia up the stairs and through the doorway of the darkened bedroom. The long sweep of her white satin skirts cascaded over his arm. Her veil was a gossamer cloud that clung to his sleeve.

He put her down on the wide bed in a tumble of satin and silk and went to the dresser. She curled up against the bedpost and watched him remove his cuff links. He took off his white shirt and then he removed the bottle of champagne from the ice bucket that sat on a stand.

The cork made the appropriately cheerful sound when it

came out of the bottle. Sam poured two glasses full of bubbling champagne and carried them both back across the room to the bed. He handed one to Virginia.

"To us," he said softly.

"To us." She smiled.

They did not take their eyes off each other as they drank the toast to their future. When Virginia had drained her glass, Sam took it from her and put it down beside his on the nightstand.

She saw the steady glow of love and happiness in his eyes when he turned back to her. She knew that he saw the same expression mirrored in her own gaze.

She slid off the bed and got to her feet. He reached out to lift the veil from her hair. She turned her back to him. He kissed the nape of her neck and went to work on the tiny buttons that secured her gown.

A thrill of pleasure went through her when the bodice of the dress fell to her waist. Sam put his arms around her from behind and cupped her breasts. His thumbs grazed across her nipples. He bent his head and kissed the side of her throat.

"I love you," he said.

She leaned back against him, savoring the warm, sleek feel of his bare chest. "I love you."

A moment later, the frothy gown cascaded into a pool at her feet. He unbuckled his belt. When she turned around, she found him ready for her, his hard body fiercely aroused. He picked her up again and settled her against the pillows. She reached for him with a kind of hunger she had never known.

He crushed her into the soft bedding, his mouth hot and deeply sensual on her skin. All of her senses opened at his touch, the paranormal ones as well as the physical. Effervescent, invisible psi energy hummed in the air that surrounded them. She knew it came from both of them, sparked by their passion and fueled by their pleasure.

Sam took his time with the lovemaking, crafting a slow,

sensual dance. She felt his mouth on her breasts, his teeth light and tantalizing on her taut nipples. She kissed his shoulder, using her own teeth in ways that made him murmur husky, sexy threats.

When, eventually, he did retaliate, she wanted to scream with delight. But she made no sound because he had stolen her very breath.

He parted her legs, settled himself between them, and forged slowly, deeply into her. She sank her nails into the hard contours of his muscled back and gloried in the full, heavy heat of his erection.

He eased himself partway out of her channel and then pressed forward again. The intense, impossibly stretched sensation was almost too much. She lifted herself against him, silently demanding that he move more quickly.

But he only laughed softly in the darkness and whispered wicked things that exacerbated the sensual torment.

Finally she could not stand it any longer. She pushed against his chest. His eyes gleamed as he allowed himself to be rolled onto his back.

She came down on top of him, fitting herself to him, kissing his chest and his throat, riding him with a wild abandon that carried them both into the heart of pure ecstasy.

A long time later, she came awake, aware that Sam was not asleep. She stirred and stretched and drew her toes up along his leg.

"Something wrong?" she asked.

"No." His arm tightened around her. "I was just thinking about that place where we hid out while I recovered from the burn."

"The zoo?"

"The more I think about it, the more I think that maybe it wasn't a zoo."

She shrugged. "A down-market apartment complex or a

cheap hotel. Maybe a prison, as you suggested. I doubt if anyone will ever know for certain, even when the experts get through untangling all the traps."

"True, but there is one explanation for the chamber that we overlooked. It fits with everything we experienced while we were in it, and it explains a lot."

She propped herself on her elbow and looked down at him. "What's that?"

"Maybe what we stumbled into was a Harmonic graveyard."

For a moment she could not believe she had heard him correctly. And then the implications hit her. Her mouth went dry.

"You think it was a *cemetery?*"

"That would account for all the small chambers," he said seriously.

"Graves and crypts." She shuddered. "Good grief. Now that you mention it—"

"It would also account for the weird feeling you got from the traps that guarded the cubicles. Maybe they were set as warnings against disturbing the dead."

"But that fountain room and the little antechamber off of it," she interrupted quickly. "Why wasn't it trapped?"

"Probably because it wasn't an actual grave site. It may have been a meditation chamber or a viewing room. Or it could have been the place where the caskets were displayed for sale, for all we know."

"Aaargh." She flopped back on the pillow. "Do you think we really spent Halloween in an alien graveyard?"

"I think there's a good chance that we did, yes."

She stared at the ceiling. "Kind of boggles the mind." Abruptly she sat up amid the sheets. "But what about that strange energy storm that Chaz triggered when he untangled one of the traps? And those things that we saw drifting past the window. You don't suppose they were—'' She broke off, unable to put the thought into words.

Sam smiled slightly. "Real ghosts?"

"No." She shook her head violently. "I absolutely refuse to believe that. The only ghosts are unstable dissonance energy manifestations. UDEMs. Composed of ambient psi energy. There is no such thing as real ghosts."

"Whatever you say." He threaded his fingers through her hair. "Who am I to argue with an expert such as yourself?"

"Definitely not real ghosts," she reiterated very forcefully. Then she frowned. "But about that antechamber off the fountain room."

"What about it?"

"If it was a funeral room or some sort of viewing chamber, then that big chest where we . . . where we—''

"Where we made love for the first time?"

"It must have been a—''

Sam grinned. "Yeah, I think it might have been a casket or a sarcophagus."

She swallowed. "We did it on top of a casket? Our first time together took place in an alien funeral parlor? On top of a *coffin?*''

"I'm pretty sure it was empty," Sam said. "There was no trap, remember?"

"That's not the point. What am I supposed to tell our grandchildren when they ask us about our first real romantic date? That you took me to an alien cemetery and made wild, passionate love to me on top of a *sarcophagus?*''

Sam roared with laughter and eased her onto her back. He lowered himself until he covered her body with his own. Then he braced his arms on either side of her head and looked down at her with eyes that gleamed with sensual amusement.

"Maybe we ought to make it our own, private Halloween tradition," he suggested. "We could hunt up a new alien graveyard every year."

"Don't even *think* about it."

He smiled slowly. "Then what do you say we get busy on creating some children so that one day we'll have those grandchildren you mentioned a minute ago."

"At last, a truly brilliant idea." She wrapped her arms around his neck and urged his mouth down to hers.

He kissed her until she stopped thinking about Halloween and graveyards and alien sarcophagi; until she could think of nothing else except their love and the future that they would build together.

Return to the fascinating and dangerous world of
Harmony!

The *New York Times* Bestselling Author

Jayne Ann Krentz

writing as

Jayne Castle

AFTER GLOW
0-515-13694-8

Licensed para-archaeologist Lydia Smith has built a
promising career in the academic world by digging
into history. When faced with holes in her own past,
Lydia must use all of her skills to unearth
the secret of what happened in order to
protect the life she's worked so hard to rebuild,
including her marriage to one of the most dangerous
men on Harmony—Emmet London.

Also available in paperback
AFTER DARK
0-515-12902-X

**Available wherever books are sold or at
penguin.com**

JAYNE ANN
KRENTZ

The *New York Times* Bestseller

TRUTH
OR
DARE

First time in paperback

JOVE

Catch all the
Hot Shots

Six quick reads from
six of your favorite bestselling authors!

Magic in the Wind
by **Christine Feehan**
0-425-20863-X

Midnight in Death by **J.D. Robb**
0-425-20881-8

Spellbound by **Nora Roberts**
0-515-14077-5

Dragonswan by **Sherrilyn Kenyon**
0-515-14079-1

Immortality by **Maggie Shayne**
0-515-14078-3

J864